Praise for the work of Manuel Ramos

"Somewhere down a dark alley, a blinding freeway, or sitting at a splintered table in a public park, sits one of Manuel Ramos' heroes. He is a disbarred lawyer, a defrocked priest, or a desperate woman. Ramos, a lawyer in some former life, tells stories of the street in an unmistakably noir style. He has heard it all, and his characters act it out. Sometimes, justice is achieved. Other times, not. The author of eight novels, Ramos sings *pochismo* jazz."
—Kathleen Alcalá, author of *The Desert Remembers My Name: On Family and Writing*, on *The Skull of Pancho Villa and Other Stories*

"The Godfather of Chicano noir hits us hard with this collection. Great range, dark visions, and lots of mojo—much of it bad to the bone. A fine book!"
—Luis Alberto Urrea, author of *The Hummingbird's Daughter*, on *The Skull of Pancho Villa and Other Stories*

"As invigorating as a dip in a Rocky Mountain stream."
—*Mystery Scene* on *Desperado: A Mile High Noir*

"A dark mix of North Denver gangsters and Catholicism, but it's [the] setting that really grips readers. Nostalgia is combined with reality . . . Ramos gets it right."
—*Denver Post* on *Desperado: A Mile High Noir*

"A very impressive debut."
—*Los Angeles Times* on *The Ballad of Rocky Ruiz*

"A thickly atmospheric first novel—with just enough mystery to hold together a powerfully elegi ... ir of the heady early days of Chicano activism."
—*Kirkus I* ... *Ruiz*

"Ramos succeeds brilliantly i ... form a seamlessly entertaining novel [w... ...eeply etched with admirable brevity and skill."
—*Publishers Weekly,* starred review, on *Blues for ... Buffalo*

"Ramos's finely crafted tales contribute a welcome Hispanic voice to the mystery genre."

—*Publishers Weekly* on *The Last Client of Luis Montez*

"Ramos tells a gripping story with panache and humor, offering an inventive plot, a cast of appealingly oddball characters, and a refreshing and likable hero."

—*Booklist* on *The Last Client of Luis Montez*

"Noir fans won't want to miss *Moony's Road to Hell*, by Denver attorney Manuel Ramos."

—*Publishers Weekly* on *Moony's Road to Hell*

SKULL OF Pancho Villa

AND OTHER STORIES

MANUEL RAMOS

Arte Público Press
Houston, Texas

The Skull of Pancho Villa and Other Stories is funded in part by grants from the city of Houston through the Houston Arts Alliance.

Recovering the past, creating the future

Arte Público Press
University of Houston
4902 Gulf Fwy, Bldg 19, Rm 100
Houston, Texas 77204-2004

Cover design by Mora Des!gn
Cover image by Mercedes Hernández

Ramos, Manuel.
[Short stories. Selections]
The Skull of Pancho Villa and other stories / by Manuel Ramos.
p cm
ISBN 978-1-55885-808-4 (alk. paper)
I. Title.
PS3568.A4468A6 2015
813'.54—dc23

2015003063
CIP

∞ The paper used in this publication meets the requirements of the American National Standard for Information Sciences—Permanence of Paper for Printed Library Materials, ANSI Z39.48-1984.

15 16 17 18 19 20 21 10 9 8 7 6 5 4 3 2 1

TABLE OF CONTENTS

LOVERS

CHICANISMO

PUBLISHING HISTORY

"Backup" originally published in *You Don't Have a Clue: Latino Mystery Stories for Teens.* Sarah Cortez, ed. Arte Público Press, 2011.

"Bad Haircut Day" originally published in *Crimespree Magazine*, #9, 2005.

"Fence Busters" originally published in *The Rocky Mountain News*, 2008, reprinted in *A Dozen on Denver*, Fulcrum, 2009.

Four lines used as an epigraph from "HOWL" from *Collected Poems 1947-1980* by Allen Ginsberg. Copyright © 1955 by Allen Ginsberg. Reprinted by permission of HarperCollins Publishers.

"If We Had Been Dancing" originally published in *Disturbing the Peace: Writing by Colorado Attorneys*. Denver and Colorado Bar Associations, 2001.

"Kite Lesson" originally published in *Upper Larimer Arts & Times*, 1987.

"La Visión de Mi Madre" originally published as "His Mother's Image" in *Southwest Tales: A Contemporary Collection.* Alurista and Rojas-Urista, eds. Maize Press, 1986, and reprinted in *Where Past Meets Present: Modern Colorado Short Stories.* Hemesath, ed. University Press of Colorado, 1994.

"Murder Movie" originally published in *Voices of Mexico*, Issue 65, 2003.

"Neighborhood Watch" originally published in *New Mystery*, Volume VII, No. 2, 2000.

"No Hablo Inglés" originally published in *Hardluckstories.com*, 2006.

"Sentimental Value" originally published in *The Cocaine Chronicles.* Phillips and Tervalon, eds. Akashic Books, 2005, 2011.

"The 405 Is Locked Down" originally published in *Latinos in Lotusland.* Daniel A. Olivas, ed. Bilingual Press, 2008.

"The Scent of Terrified Animals" originally published in *Saguaro,* Volume 6, 1990.

"The Skull of Pancho Villa" originally published in *Hit List: The Best of Latino Mystery.* Sarah Cortez and Liz Martínez, eds. Arte Público Press, 2009.

"The Smell of Onions" originally published in *Rocky Mountain Arsenal of the Arts*, 1989, reprinted as a poem in *The Lineup: Poems on Crime*, Issue 2, 2009.

"The Truth Is" originally published in *Pearl Street Press*, 1989.

"When the Air Conditioner Quit" originally published in *Crimespree Magazine*, #51, 2013.

"White Devils and Cockroaches" originally published by *Westword*, 1986.

INTRODUCTION

These stories span the years 1986 through 2014. "White Devils and Cockroaches" first appeared in *Westword* because it placed second in the annual fiction contest that the magazine sponsored back then. It was my first published story. The collection includes one poem, "The Smell of Onions" and one story that previously appeared in a collection of young adult mystery fiction, "Backup." "Fence Busters" was selected as one of the stories for the *Rocky Mountain News'* unique project of showcasing Denver fiction as a way of celebrating both the paper's and the city's 150th anniversaries. A quartet of *ficción rápida*—"Texas Afternoon," "When Pigs Fly and Monkeys Talk," "2012," and "Honesty Is the Best Policy"—were posted on the literary blog *La Bloga* in different versions and appear here for the first time as traditionally published pieces.

The tag Chicano Noir applies to some of the stories, as does hard-boiled to others, while still others have no label other than "story." A few are predecessors to longer works. The attorney in "White Devils and Cockroaches," González, morphed over the years into Luis Móntez, the protagonist in five of my novels. "Kite Lesson" became a chapter in *King of the Chicanos*, while "The Skull of Pancho Villa" launched my character Gus Corral, and that story is now Chapter 5 in *Desperado: A Mile High Noir*.

There is a story about each of these stories.

For Roberto Santos, Diego Ramos, and Gabriel White—
three men who, by doing some of their growing up in
our house, enriched our lives.

BASIC BLACK

NO HABLO INGLÉS

The lone ray of sunshine streaming through a crease in the dirt-stained window caught the corner of my eye and my head throbbed. A splinter of pain lodged itself in my eyeball. I sucked on a Tecate and a slice of lime whose rind had brown spots. I couldn't remember the name of the joint in Juárez that had produced the hangover.

"So, what's the deal, Manolo? Can you do any kind of lawyerin', or is it like, you know, over for good?"

Nick knew I didn't talk about my disbarment, but he asked crap all the time.

"Nick," I answered, looking him straight in his blood-shot eyes. "Can you still say Mass? Give communion with the watered-down tequila you serve?"

He said something like "fuck you" and turned his attention to wiping the far side of the bar with a gray, stiff rag.

I dropped two bucks and eased out of the clammy, musty-smelling air of Nick's Cave and into the white glare and oven heat of another El Paso morning.

I hated the town, but that wasn't El Paso's fault. I hated myself and that meant I hated wherever I woke up. That summer it was El Paso.

I waited in the congestion and noise that led to the Santa Fe International Bridge, sweating through my shirt, as lost as if I had been abandoned naked in the desert. I lit up my last American Spirit and crossed the street when the traffic slowed for a minute.

The diner was busy and I hesitated at the door until an old Mexican wearing a packing-house hardhat pushed himself from his table, stuck a few dollars under his fork and walked out with a toothpick hanging from his lip. I took his place before it had been cleared by the young Mexican busboy. He grimaced at me when he came to pick up the greasy plate and stained coffee cup but he didn't say anything. He also didn't wipe the crumbs off the tabletop.

I opened my notebook and stared at the pages of the great Chicano novel that I had decided I would write that summer, seeing as how I didn't have much else to do. My words didn't make sense. Some of the sentences trailed off the edge of the page. I must have been drunk when I wrote most of them.

The waitress cleared her throat and I realized that she stood next to me.

"What you want, Manolo?" she asked in Spanish.

I answered, in English, "Eggs and chorizo, coffee. One of those grilled jalapeños."

She said, "Whatever," in English, and appeared to run away from me.

What the hell, I thought. We used to be friends. At least one night not that long ago we were really good friends. Why'd she act like that?

The door opened and hot air rushed in. I smelled sweat and grease.

"You the lawyer?" The accent was thick but the words were clear.

She was small, pretty, dark and afraid.

"No, I'm not a lawyer."

"The man at the bar across the street." Her eyes were wide and her lips trembled. "He said the lawyer came in here and that he would be wearing a white shirt. You're the only man in here with a white shirt."

I looked at the diner's other customers and she was right.

"But that doesn't make me a lawyer."

Tears welled up in her eyes but nothing rolled down her cheeks. She backed out of the diner, looked up and down the street, then raced in the direction of Mexico.

The frayed cuffs of my shirt had a thin border of dirt. I fingered the empty space where a missing button belonged.

The waitress appeared with my coffee. I stubbed out what was left of my smoke and carefully placed it in my shirt pocket. I said, "This used to be a very good shirt. I wore it in court. I used to kick butt in this shirt."

She rolled her eyes and shook her head.

"You are so full of shit, Manolo." She hurried away again.

I pulled out my wallet and was relieved to see the twenty. For an instant I thought I might have left it all in Juárez. I had more back in my room, in the so-called safe, but I understood that it was running out. The dregs of what I had managed to salvage from the Colorado Supreme Court's order to reimburse my former clients couldn't last more than a few weeks.

I finished the breakfast, except for the chile, and drank several cups of coffee and finally left when the waitress stopped coming by. I crossed the street again and forced myself into Nick's.

Two men sat at the bar, dressed in cowboy hats and shirts, jeans and boots. They talked loudly with the speeded-up rhythm of Mexicans who have been too long on the American side of the border. I sat in one of the booths, almost in darkness. My eyes took their time adjusting to the change in light and when Nick asked me what I wanted, I could barely make out his silhouette.

"Just a beer. Tecate."

Nick had a CD player behind the bar and I thought I heard Chalino Sánchez. The slightly off-key, high-pitched voice of the martyred wannabe filled the bar with a lament about bad luck with young women. An accordion, a tinny cymbal, brass horns and drums emphasized the singer's misery.

When Nick came back and set down the beer can, I grabbed his wrist.

"What did that woman want, Nick? Why did you send her to me?"

"The fuck I know? She said she was lookin' for the Mexican-American lawyer. There's only one asshole I know that fits that description. I told her you was across the street." He jerked his arm free of my grip.

"There are plenty of Chicano lawyers in this town. Too many. What made you think she wanted me?"

He had turned away. He stopped, looked down at me. "She didn't have any money."

I rubbed my temples, took my time with the beer.

The two men at the bar stood up, arguing and shoving each other. Nick shouted at them to get the hell out, but they ignored him. I squeezed myself into the corner of the booth and watched as one of the men pulled a knife from somewhere and slashed at the other man. Drops of blood appeared on the slashed man's shirt. He slapped his chest with his left hand. Nick grabbed the man with the knife, knocked the weapon free and wrestled him to the door. Curses and shouts filled the bar and whoever had followed Chalino Sánchez on Nick's CD player was drowned out by the familiar sound of men fighting in a bar. The wounded man stumbled to the doorway just as Nick tossed out the knife-wielder.

The former friends stood about two feet apart, in the middle of the sidewalk. The cut man's fingers gripped his chest and were covered with blood. The other man grinned. He finally laughed and walked away. His bloody companion slowly followed.

"Look at this floor!" Nick shouted. "Goddamn blood spots. Now I got to get the bleach." His face was red and a thin line of blood traced his jawline.

I stood up from the booth and walked to where Nick examined the floor.

"That woman, Nick? What was her problem?"

"You fuckin' kiddin' me? Why didn't you ask her yourself? She said somethin' about her sister. Usual shit. Christ." He shook his head and disappeared into a closet. I heard him banging a bucket and shaking out a mop.

I made it back to my room and laid down on the bed. I sweated for an hour, listening to the traffic in the street below, smelling the traffic. I blotted out everything else about the room, the town, the day. When I decided to leave, I took off the white shirt and replaced it with a blue shirt that I had never worn in court.

I walked toward the border, to the bridge where anyone with a quarter can cross into Mexico unless the bridge is closed because of a bomb threat. There had been such a threat the day before and that had been my excuse to stay in Juárez longer than I had planned. That's what I had told myself at dawn when I tripped on the American side of the bridge and had trouble getting up.

I finished the butt saved from breakfast and scanned the line of people walking into Mexico. I looked over the vendors with their trinkets and gewgaws, tried to recognize the face of the small, dark, pretty and frightened woman who had wanted to talk to a North American lawyer about her sister.

"You ever been to the shrine of Santa Muerte?" The boy asking the question had straight, thick hair, like some kind of Indian, and the darkest eyes I had ever seen on a human being. One of the eyes was crooked and it distracted me so that when he spoke I thought he was talking to someone behind and to the left of me.

"Saint Death? I don't think so. I don't have time, and I don't have any money."

"Hey, *pocho*, I don't want your money. I'm talking about La Santísima Muerte, the only real saint, the only one worth praying to anyway." His English was good, better than my Spanish, so we talked in English. "She only promises what she will actually deliver, and she treats everyone the same—rich, poor, Mexican, gringo."

The boy wasn't going anywhere, so I asked a question. "What kind of shrine is this?"

"A special place. A girl got killed there and when her mother found the body, it was covered in roses that bloomed for weeks after. Now people go there to ask for help."

"Why would I want to see this shrine?"

"You're looking for something. Ain't nothing she can't help find, because everything and everyone all end up with her anyway."

I used my handkerchief to wipe the sweat from the back of my neck. The monogrammed MT had faded from its original deep royal blue to a pallid gray. I stuffed the handkerchief back in my pocket.

"Tell me, boy, you think someone who is looking for a lost sister might go to the shrine?"

He smiled and exposed gaps in his teeth.

"She already has, *pocho*. About an hour ago. I took her myself."

"Show me."

"Two American dollars."

"You said you didn't want money."

"That was before you wanted something."

I gave him the two bills and I thought how that could buy me a cold beer at Nick's.

The boy veered from the bridge and we dashed across the street. He scrambled into an alley, then another, turned back and headed to the outskirts of the town. I sweated like I had a fever, and my breath came hard and fast before we ended up in the basement of a broken-down apartment building.

We walked along a narrow concrete hallway that smelled of *copal* and marigolds. Candles lit the way into a dark, damp corner of the basement. Hundreds of candles. The boy kept walking, didn't look at me, didn't say a word.

The statute of the saint of death standing on a makeshift altar looked like the grim reaper to me. Various offerings surrounded it—food, money, photographs, pieces of clothing. There were about a dozen people standing or kneeling around the altar and they mumbled prayers that I couldn't understand. I walked around the small room and looked for the woman who had confronted me in the diner, but the only light came from candles and the people kept their faces down and hidden behind mantillas and dusty hats. I didn't see the woman.

I wanted to ask the boy to take me back but he was gone. Some in the crowd started to leave. I followed them down what I thought was the same candled hallway. They murmured to each other, stayed close and kept looking over their shoulders at me. They moved faster and I had to exert myself to keep up with them. They turned a corner, but when I followed, they were gone. I was in another small room without candles, without any light. I heard Spanish words and phrases and the brassy, loud grating music of a Mexican band. Then I heard words in a language I did not recognize and music that I had never heard before.

I waited. A few minutes passed, then another group of people from the shrine entered the room and shifted sharply to my left, toward an opening that I had not seen.

I said, "Wait, show me the way. I'm lost."

An old woman wearing a black shawl over her waist-long gray hair stopped. She looked at me and said, "*No hablo inglés*."

I repeated my request in Spanish but she shrugged and trudged into the darkness. I followed the sounds of her footsteps. After a few minutes I heard nothing but I kept walking in the dark, sometimes feeling my way around corners, until I found myself in the stench and heat of a deserted El Paso alley.

An hour later I was back in Nick's, drinking a beer.

"They're on their way to lose their cherries, across the bridge." Nick smirked at the boys at the end of the bar. I assumed he talked to me because the underage boys were the only other people in the bar and he must have figured that he would be less susceptible to being shut down if he avoided them, even though he served them shots of tequila.

I didn't have a response.

"They found another one," Nick said.

"Another what?" I asked, but I knew what he was talking about.

"A dead woman, out in the desert by the wire. Cut up like the others. Been missin' for weeks."

"How many's that?"

"There's no official count. Hundreds, thousands. Like that girl the woman was lookin' for. Missin' for weeks."

"How do you know that?"

He frowned. "She told me, what d'ya think? Anyway, she's lookin' for her missin' sister, in Juárez and El Paso. What the hell you think that means?"

I got up to leave. "Why would she want to talk to me about that? I can't do anything about her missing sister."

"Come on, Manolo. You can't do anything about anybody's problems. Remember? You screwed that up, as I heard you explain one night."

"Yeah, yeah. I screwed it up. So why would she want to talk to me?"

He shrugged, twisted his bar rag. "She heard about the American lawyer. That means somethin' to some people. She heard that the lawyer hung out in the bars. She tried to track you down. She thought you might be able to help, maybe you knew somebody, maybe you heard somethin'. She had nowhere else to go, no one else to talk to." He tossed his rag under the bar. "Dammit, Manolo, I don't know."

He walked over to the boys and said, "How about another one for the road?"

They laughed uneasily and moved away when he tried to put his arm around the shoulders of the shortest kid.

I left Nick and his dingy bar and his ugly reputation and swore that I was done with all of it. I had walked about two blocks when I saw her. She leaned against a brick wall, the side of a building that housed a *mercado* where every week tourists spent thousands of dollars on useless souvenirs and phony mementos.

She cringed when she saw me.

"I can't help. I don't know anything, anyone." I used my hands to help my explanation.

She cocked her head. Her face was smudged with the tracks of the tears that had finally flowed.

She reached into her thin jacket and waved a small gun. I shook my head and put my hands in front of me, but she pulled the trigger. The shot made me jump, then I fell to the ground. The pain in my shoulder wrenched my torso. I twisted on the grimy sidewalk.

I gurgled one word: "What?"

"*No hablo inglés*," she said. She dropped the gun and walked away.

I sat up, but dizziness bent me forward and I slumped to the sidewalk.

The hospital released me two days later. I left El Paso and returned to Denver.

When it snows, my shoulder aches, and I smell *copal* and marigolds.

TEXAS AFTERNOON

The back of his neck itched from the sun. He scratched but the rough skin of his fingers did nothing to help.

The summer haze made him squint. Heat vapors wiggled against the horizon. His hat slumped around his ears, and his horse moved to the torpid rhythm of the desert—slow, steady, dying. The pistol hanging from his belt was hot to the touch. He considered using it one last time. The long ride had to end.

A ray of light from the top of the dune pierced his eyes. He slipped from the horse and rolled to a boulder. Streaks of pain ran from his lungs to his groin. Dirt filled his mouth. He pulled the gun.

"Mateo! Surrender or you die today! *Vamos a matarlo.*"

He smiled at the broken Spanish. Did they think he didn't understand? They wanted him dead, that's all he needed to know.

"*Aquí 'stoy*. Come and get me."

He licked his cracked lips. Breathing burned his lungs. A broken rib when the crazy horse kicked him. Spooked by the gunshots, but what an animal! Ran until her heart gave out.

He aimed his pistol at the light. He waited to see their hats.

Mercedes. Carlos. María. His memories had become names only. He could not see their faces anymore, or hear the music in their voices. He prayed their names to himself a hundred times a day. He chased their ghosts as the men chased him. Outrunning the men through the arroyo, then the hills, and now the desert. He shouted the names and heard the lonely echoes and believed that he had lost his mind.

He had enough. He stood up.

"*¡Ya basta!*"

The first shot exploded the dirt in front of his ragged boots. The second whizzed by his ear. He fell to his knees before the third one tore through his shoulder. He dropped his gun and shouted his memories.

He heard a rattlesnake's warning, a hawk's squeal, the hot wind gasp. He opened his eyes. Blood soaked the remains of his shirt.

He struggled to his feet and stumbled to the dune.

The blood of three men streamed over sand and rocks. Across the ridge he saw the Comanches. They laughed at him, turned their horses and disappeared below the haze. He picked up a dead man's canteen and poured water down his throat. He choked, sputtered, coughed. He prayed the names of his memories.

—WHEN THE AIR CONDITIONER QUIT—

When the air conditioner quit, Torres shot it. The bullet bounced around the machine's innards like an insane pinball.

"I don't have time for this shit," he said.

Juanita rushed into the room. "Jesus! What the hell was that?"

"Damn thing's broke. I put it out of its misery." He laughed the horse laugh that she hated. Sweat already flowed down his back.

The gray dented machine sported an ugly hole in its side. It hung crookedly in the window. A thin spiral of smoke rose from its louvered vents.

"You dumb son-of-a-bitch. Now what're we gonna do? It'll hit a hunnerd again today. You think of that before you pulled the trigger?"

"I tole you it's broke. Useless. You said it yourself."

"I said it was goin' out. Big difference."

"Well, it went out. It stopped. Nothin' but hot air comin' from it. Stinkin' up the place. You must'a smelled it."

"So you shot it? Are you crazy?"

He grinned at her and scratched the back of his ear with the barrel of the gun. "You don't even have to ask, do you?"

She flipped him the bird, returned to the kitchen. At least her fan moved the cooked air while she cleaned a pot in the sink.

Torres tucked the gun in the waistband of his sweat pants and covered it with his T-shirt. He needed a drink.

"I'll kill somebody if I stay here," he said to the stuffed owl. He rubbed his hands through his hair. "I'm taking the pickup into town," he shouted. "I'll be back for supper." He looked in the direction of the kitchen.

"Good riddance," Juanita said. "Don't kill any tractors on your way. Or mailboxes. Damn things might shoot back." She laughed and shook her head.

Torres laughed, too. That's what he liked about Juanita.

She almost added that he should look for a job, but the smell from the air conditioner cautioned her and she bit her tongue. He did what he could, she reasoned. What with the recession and all.

The pickup practically drove itself along the rutted dirt road for the five miles into Dexter. Torres hummed along to Hank Williams, Jr. "All my rowdy friends have settled down . . . "

He had money for a few drinks. Robbie Claxton, over in Roswell, finally paid him for the briefcase of weed from Albuquerque. Took him long enough. Juanita didn't know he'd been paid but he'd work it out with her. Tell her, "I'll put somethin' away for a new air conditioner, get that dog you want and then we'll see what comes up."

The bulge of his wallet pressed against his butt. Five hundred dollars for a day's worth of work. Not even work. Driving, mostly. Watching for cops, staying cool, under the radar. Picking up and delivering the package. Nothing to it. Life should always be so easy.

He rubbed the American flag tattoo on his right bicep.

For a hot minute he thought about making a run to the border. In the old days, with five hundred bucks in his pocket, he would've disappeared for a week. Easy to do in El Paso, Juárez. The things he'd seen, no one believed. Some of it he wanted to forget.

He drove along quiet South Lincoln Avenue until he saw the faded sign that years before blinked "Bar" and then "Café." These days it stuck on "Bar." He stopped on the patch of soft asphalt that passed for a parking lot.

The Hi-Way offered nothing more than beer, strong whiskey, air conditioning and a jukebox with country and Tejano music. That was enough for Torres and the four other customers.

"It's like a ghost town out there," he said to Cole, the bartender. "I didn't see nobody."

"Too damn hot," Cole said. "And there's no work. It's been so dead I've been thinkin' of stayin' closed until the weekend."

Torres adjusted to the semi-darkness by squinting. He ordered a shot of whiskey and a beer back. He chugged the shot, sipped the beer. When he caught Cole's eye, he ordered another shot. The second shot lasted longer than the first.

By the time three empty beers sat on the bar he'd forgotten his promise to be home for dinner.

"Hey, Torres. How's it hangin'?" Claxton's younger brother slapped him on the back. Torres flinched under the sting of the slap. Dickie smelled like cigarettes and whiskey.

"Hey, Dickie. What you doin' round here? I thought you was away at school."

Torres moved his whiskey closer. Dickie was a big kid, like every Claxton. Had that wild red hair they all carried. Quite a coincidence to run into Dickie Claxton. In the Hi-Way, of all places.

"That's for suckers. I got more important things to do, know what I mean?"

"Yeah, sure. You here with Robbie?"

"Nah. On my own. Just checkin' out the scene here in beautiful downtown Dexter. These Dexter women are good ole country girls, you know?"

"Yeah. I guess." Torres didn't see one woman in the bar.

Dickie laughed. Torres tried to laugh but he choked on his beer. He knew about the rape charge and getting tossed from New Mexico State. Everyone knew. The paper made it front page news. No one brought it up, not to Dickie or his brother, that was for sure.

Torres finished his beer. He decided to leave. He opened his wallet to lay money on the bar. Dickie grabbed his wrist.

"Hey, where you goin'? The party's just started. You need to catch up. I'm way ahead. Let me buy you a drink."

Torres twisted his arm from Dickie's grasp. "I gotta go. Juanita's waitin'. There's some work to do around the house."

"Your shack, you mean? That place needs a lot of work, bud. What could you possibly do that would fix it?"

"The air conditioner's been actin' up."

"You know about air conditioners? I thought you was a roofer. What the hell you know about air conditioners?"

Dickie stepped away from the bar. He stood over Torres, at least six inches. His eyes fixed on the wallet.

Torres shoved the wallet in his back pocket. The movement lifted his shirt and Dickie saw the gun. Dickie shuffled back to the bar.

"But if you gotta go . . . " Dickie's voice trailed off.

"Yeah. I gotta go. Maybe next time."

"Whatever." He turned to Torres. "Robbie paid you? I was supposed to do that job for him, you know? But Robbie couldn't wait. Your good luck, eh?"

"Do what I have to. Need the work. Your brother will have more for you. He always does."

"Yeah. Maybe." Dickie stared down his beer bottle.

Robbie was okay, a good guy really, but Dickie was over the edge.

Torres walked out of the bar into the blazing sunshine. He swayed from the booze and the heat. The daytime glare blinded him. He stopped to get his bearings. Someone stood behind him. He tried to move out of the way. A fist slammed into his kidney. Torres fell forward on the asphalt. The gun slipped out of his pants.

"The wallet. Or I kick your face in."

Torres struggled but Dickie's boot dug into his throat. He pulled the wallet from his pocket. Dickie snatched it. The younger Claxton stepped back, hesitated, then punched Torres on the chin. He walked away, easy and slow.

Torres rubbed his jaw, tasted blood. He picked up the gun, aimed it at Dickie's back. He flashed on the air conditioner.

A shadow crossed his face. Robbie Claxton blocked the sun.

"You ain't gonna do that, Torres. Give me the gun. I'll get your money back."

Torres handed over the gun. Robbie held it like it was a glass of water and he didn't want to spill a drop. He moved quickly after his brother.

Torres sat on his haunches.

The Claxtons disappeared around the corner of the bar. Torres heard shouting, a few grunts. He thought he should do something. The empty street stretched away from the building. A white haze of summer light beat down on him.

He jerked his head when he heard the gunshot. A dog barked across the street. No one came out of the bar.

Torres stood up. He leaned against his pickup, his hands in his pockets, his mind locked down. Robbie stumbled into view. Blood oozed from his chest. His bloody hand held the wallet.

"Take the goddam money and go home."

Claxton fell to his knees. Blood quickly covered his shirt. Tires squealed from behind the building. Torres ran into the bar and hollered for Cole to call 9-1-1.

He ran back outside followed by the bar's customers. He did what he could but Robbie Claxton was dead by the time the ambulance screeched into the parking lot.

The cops arrived at the same time. They ran around for a few minutes before they settled into a routine. One cop crossed the street and knocked on the door of a house. The cop in charge questioned the men from the bar. He paid special attention to Torres.

"I had a drink," Torres told him. "When I was getting into my truck, Robbie come around the building, bleeding." The cop took notes as Torres talked. "He must'a been in a fight in the back. I didn't see anyone else. I tried to stop the bleeding but it didn't do no good. Got blood all over my hands." He showed his hands to the cop.

"You got some on your lip," the cop said.

Torres rubbed his chin and lips with the back of his hand.

"I knowed this guy since high school," he said. The cop nodded.

Torres didn't say anything about Dickie, nor that Dickie drove a red F-150 with chrome wheels. How could he explain five hundred dollars?

The ambulance men loaded the body on a stretcher and covered it with a blanket. A dark red stain flared over the white cloth. The men lifted the stretcher. Torres watched his wallet fall like a wounded bird dropping from the sky. One of the ambulance guys picked it up and handed it to the cop. The cop thumbed through it. "This Claxton's?"

"Don't know," Torres said. "Didn't see it before. It was on him, right?"

"Under him. No money or I.D. Looks like he was robbed. I'll give it to his widow."

An hour later the cop said Torres could leave. "I hope you get the guy," Torres said.

He cleaned up the best he could in the bar's restroom. No soap, only a few paper towels.

His pickup started right up and he sped through the streets. He stomped the pedal when he swerved into the dirt road. The cab suffocated him. He kept the windows up because of the dust. His hands sweated on the steering wheel. Blood and sweat stained his T-shirt and pants.

He couldn't stop thinking about what happened between the Claxton brothers. And his money. He thought so hard and deep that he didn't see the red truck until he was about a hundred yards from the house.

Then he saw Juanita hunched over in the doorway. She didn't look right.

OUTPOST DUTY

The mountain air stimulated Corporal Martínez and it dawned on him that every sound, every smell was intense and vibrant. A reflection of the importance of his job, he thought. "Outpost duty is not so bad," he said to himself as he huddled near the campfire. "Except for the pig private."

He stared at the lump on the other side of the fire. The man infuriated him, almost made him physically sick. He was filthy, grotesque, and he smelled. Martínez knew the private was in the federal army only because these were desperate times. Revolutions popped up in the countryside almost every month, or so the newspapers reported, and the government conscripts were men who had little value except that they could serve as bodies, numbers to swell the ranks, ineffective as soldiers. "Private Santos should count for two. Ha!" Martínez muffled his laughter, not because of fear that he would wake the private, the man could sleep through an earthquake, but because he was, after all, on outpost duty and bandits were in the area.

His task was to watch for them. He had been selected for duty in the most advanced position the government controlled and he believed that was an honor, an opportunity created by the turbulent times that would not have come his way in peace time. He was a professional soldier, a man who thought to make the army his life's work, if only the private didn't sabotage his efforts. The private was lazy and obviously a coward. The corporal believed that only his superior military skills would save them if, indeed, they had to confront the bandits.

Martínez knew exactly what he would do when he faced the enemy. He excelled at planning. Military strategy was a specialty of his. He mapped out vast maneuvers and campaigns in his head or scratched them in the dirt. His chance would come with the clouds of dust kicked up by the bandits' horses when the historic showdown happened between the *federales* and the bandits. Martínez would make a wild dash back to the division headquarters, where he could give his valuable information to the colonel and help plan the counterattack. Martínez would impress the colonel with his well-developed military knowledge. He would be given command of a squad of crack troops, the main thrust of the offensive, and his men would shout his name in glory as he led them to victory, fame and his own promotion to colonel.

Yes, he was blessed with the gift of planning.

The routine had been the same for weeks for Martínez. He watched and waited for the enemy. He moved his outpost to avoid discovery. The days passed slowly in the worn-out countryside. The private was his first companion since the assignment had been given to him.

The mountains were unchanging, gloomy mounds of earth that reminded him of the graveyard in his home town. Impatience for action played on his concentration, and his thoughts wandered to memories of his home and family. When he thought of Antonia, her soft skin and long, thick hair, he felt a loss, a pang of homesickness. He abruptly shook his head, made the unwelcome feelings disappear. He thought again about the importance of his duty.

Where are they? Even I am tired of waiting. Why don't they come? They have to move through this valley. Maybe through one of the other arroyos. Then Hernández or García will see them, report them to headquarters, and here I'll be, stuck in nowhere with this miserable slob. That can't happen! They have to come this way! They have to!

The private snored, growled in his sleep and then rolled over like a fat bear in the zoo. Bugs crawled from under his hulk. The glow of the fire lighted up his mud-encrusted beard, testimony to his hard riding the past few days to get to the outpost. He had been in the attack at Zacatecas and then ordered to help Martínez. He dreamed of a naked woman, wanton and coarse.

Private Santos hated the army. He was a *peón*, a poor country boy with no special allegiance to the government or the rebels. He was forced to join the army and he accepted that as his fate, just as his poverty and struggle to survive were all part of life, part of the hand he had been dealt. He was taught in a week how to shoot, how to march and how to take orders and then thrown into battle against Villa's men. He killed to survive, without hatred or patriotic fervor. Now he waited in the desert, asleep and content that he would live another day.

The corporal did not affect him. The man had insane ideas about war. He obviously was ambitious, he talked high and mighty, and Santos knew that they had nothing in common. But that was life. One had to survive, that was one's obligation, one's duty.

Martínez kicked Santos' boot. "Wake up, you lazy ass! Your watch. Wake up!" He kicked the sleeping man again.

The larger man woke, slowly, and then stretched his cramped legs and arms. He leaned close to the fire in an attempt to warm his chilled bones. He grabbed his rifle and stared off into the night. He asked for coffee. "I feel like I haven't eaten for days. What I wouldn't give for some lamb *mole*, *cabrito*, *ay*, anything except beans."

Martínez threw a piece of wood on the fire. "We're lucky to have beans. If we cooked anything other than beans you can bet we'd have every bandit and coyote within ten miles sniffing around. With beans we're like every Indian around here. Anything else would be too suspicious. We have to manage with what we've got."

Santos snorted and moved his fat rear end off a rock. "You really think Villa is coming this way? You've been out here for how long, two, three weeks? Villa is long gone. He packed his men on the train and headed back north. They're probably in Juárez, maybe even the States. Long gone from around here."

"Don't say that! They'll come this way, I know it. They have to. They need to make a show of force to keep the peasants in line. If they retreat now they lose face and what little support they have. No, they'll come this way. They have to engage our troops one more time before they head north. They have to!"

"If you say so, corporal. I'll let you know if I see anything. You'll be the first to know."

Martínez could not see his smirk—the broad, toothy smile—in the darkness.

"I've got to relieve myself. I'll be back in a quarter of an hour. Watch for me." Martínez walked into the desert. The fire gave enough light for him to be seen for ten yards beyond the camp, then he was swallowed by the night.

"What an idiot!" Santos let the fire warm him. He drew a blanket tight around his shoulders and soon his eyes were heavy. He tried to focus on the horizon, but all he saw was darkness, and he fell asleep. He dreamed again of the naked woman.

Bushes hid Martínez as he squatted over the earth. Plans for elaborate military exercises filled his head as he waited for his bowels to move. He imagined leading an attack on Villa's camp. He saw himself wrestling the bandit leader to the ground and forcing him to surrender. "Mexico's savior. Long live Martínez!"

"Look at this, boys. A *federale*, bare-assed out here where the snakes and lizards could bite his balls off!"

The laughter of men surrounded Martínez before he knew he was captured. He tried to jump to his feet but he fell backwards, tripped by his pants. His naked legs clawed the air.

Martínez squealed, "What? Who? How did you?"

The men laughed again. One of them stood with a boot on the corporal's quivering belly. "How pretty this one is. It will be a shame to shoot such a handsome soldier." He poked at Martínez with his rifle. "Hey, pretty one. Want to have some fun?"

The laughter was rough and strained. The men knew they had a short time to enjoy the game, then it had to end. The war had to be fought.

Martínez tried to make sense out of what had happened. Maybe he should try to make a run for it. But the boot heel dug into his guts and he was forced to squirm in his excrement. He tried to explain. "You can't do this. You have to ride in. I have to tell the colonel. It can't be this way, my squad, the offensive, don't you see, don't you see?"

The men were silent. The time had come.

The leader handed his rifle to one of the others. He pulled a handgun from his holster and placed the barrel next to Martínez' ear. "Too bad, pretty one. We can't use crazy prisoners, we can't take any prisoners. Mother of God! What a war!"

He squeezed the trigger and Martínez died trying to make sense of it all.

Santos thought he heard a shot but his dream was too vivid to turn loose. He was deep in sleep thinking that it was one of life's unexplained ironies, and, therefore, regrettable, that dreams did not come true.

—WHITE DEVILS AND COCKROACHES—

González made a living representing crazies, weirdos, misfits, losers and plain folks who got taken. A damn good legal aid lawyer, ace attorney for the underdog, a craftsman in the courtroom with a bit of magician in his blood. That image had kept him at legal aid past the usual tour of duty.

Each morning he reminded himself he was not a burned out liberal who took up space on legal aid's payroll.

***

Joey and Pauline Maldonado had given the manager of a run down apartment building fifty dollars to hold a place for them for the beginning of March. On February 20th they showed up with a truckload of furniture. The rooms were filthy. The walls needed paint, two windows were busted, the refrigerator was broken and the lights were out. Rose, the manager, gave them a break, even though they were more than a week early. She was new. She let them unload their boxes and plastic bags in the empty rooms.

Rose later maintained they were only to store their things until the rooms were ready, but Joey and Pauline settled in without lights, windows, a refrigerator or paint. Joey and Pauline stalled Rose on the rent for a few days. Joey found a job as a dishwasher at the White Spot on Colfax and he swore he would be paid in a week. He told Gary, the owner, that the check for the first month's rent was in the mail and Gary, who should have known better, let him slide. Two weeks later Gary ordered Rose to evict the couple.

Pauline tried to explain their problem to González as he sat across the desk from her, bored with a story he had heard too many times.

She was a skinny, pockmarked white woman of twenty-three. Her lips twitched and her fingers scratched at the insides of her elbows as she described the conditions in which she was living. Yellow eyes peered through thick glasses perched on the end of her nose.

"See, me and Joey knowed they wasn't going to do what they said about the windows, so we told them they wasn't going to get the rent until we got them fixed. That really pissed off Rose, so she turned off the electricity, and ya know how cold it gets here at night. We even had some snow a few days ago and me and Joey almost froze our asses off, excuse me, but ya know what I mean, Mr. González?"

The lawyer tried not to believe her. Even so, he knew enough about Capitol Hill landlords that he was tempted to tell the wasted *gabacha* he would represent her and her old man.

"Joey's in jail, I told ya, huh? Some mistake about some old traffic tickets or somethin', I don't even know how it could happen, we only been in town a few months. We came from California, ya know? He'll get out in a few days."

He nodded and told her he would call the manager, talk to her about the heat, and then decide if he would prepare a defense so that Joey and Pauline could have their day in court.

González did not learn anything more from Rose. She insisted he had to speak with Gary but she refused to tell

González how to reach the owner. González had been through this routine before and it tipped the scales in favor of Joey and Pauline. He cut and pasted together a pleading that raised issues of implied covenants, express promises, invasion of privacy and constructive eviction. He demanded not only the return of the original fifty dollars but punitive damages as well. González could be creative when landlords tried to fool with him.

He filed the document with the court clerk, convinced Judge Kerso to waive the filing fees and set the trial for the next week. In eviction cases the wheels of justice did not turn as slowly as González preferred.

Pauline called a few days later and asked about the trial. He told her what to expect and made another appointment to prepare them. "I need to talk to Joey so he'll know what I want from him when he testifies. Make sure you bring him." She promised.

Gary Donley, a young man with plenty of money, owner of several apartment buildings, knew the eviction process better than most attorneys. He was enraged when he read the pleading González served on him.

He called legal aid and demanded to speak to González. He was on hold for almost five minutes. The receptionist was working on the bugs in the new system and Donley was one of the unfortunate souls lost in the limbo of the legal aid telephones.

"This answer is a goddamned lie! How in the hell could you sign this piece of shit! I ought to have you and those two assholes arrested for putting a fraud on the court!"

González interrupted Donley in the middle of a string of epithets that alluded to the unsavory nature of Joey's ancestry. "Look, Donley. If you can't be civil, I don't think we can discuss this. Just tell me what you know about the situation and maybe we can work something out."

And Donley did. He told González about the all-night fights between Pauline and Joey. He talked about screams from the apartment, blood on the door, and the cops who took Joey away for chasing people down the hallway with an axe. He told him about the lousy fifty bucks and that the two had knowingly moved in without any lights. He said they had heat and gas and cooked something that smelled up the building like burnt horseshit. He ended by telling González he would see him in court and they would learn then who was awarded punitive damages and "attorney fees, González. How would legal aid like to pay me a couple of thousand because one of their smart ass lawyers defended a frivolous case?" González knew legal aid would not like it, not one damn bit.

He visited Joey Maldonado in the City Jail. Joey was a short, pale Chicano with greasy hair. His eyes were dull and he talked with a slight stutter. González had a hard time picturing him chasing anybody, especially with an axe.

"Man, those p-people are crazy in that place. They barge in whenever they w-want, they threaten me and Pauline, they cut our damn extension cord we had plugged in to the outlet in the hall so we could have some f-fuckin' lights. They're animals, man. I hope we can just let the judge know about all the shit that goes on in that p-place, because I know a lot, man. That bitch, Rose, ya know the manager, she's a damn dealer. She's always tryin' to sell some shit to us, ya know, grass or some snort, even some m-m-meth. That's half the reason why they're f-fuckin' with us, ya know, we wouldn't b-buy any of her crap."

González tried to get details about the arrangement with Rose when they moved in, but Joey wanted to talk about the manager's criminal activities. González left not knowing any more than when he walked to the jail from his office.

The day before the trial Pauline called to let him know she could not make the appointment. She did not feel very well.

"And what about Joey, Pauline? Where is he?"

"He was out but he got busted again. I don't even know if he'll be out by the trial tomorrow."

"What he get arrested for?"

"Some mix-up, I don't know."

Her words were slurred. She lost her train of thought. González decided she was drunk or high on drugs. She cried. "But I'm going to fight this time, they can't push us around like this. I want a trial and I want you to be there. Okay?"

"Donley told me Joey chases people with axes, that he beats people up and that he's been trashing the place."

"No way, man. Joey ain't like that. Joey was arrested for domestic abuse. You know how it is in Colorado now. They take away the husband for domestic abuse, throw him in jail. I told them I was all right." Something burned in González's stomach. "But he don't bother nobody, except me. Gary's lying if he says Joey was arrested for hasslin' other people. Joey's only into domestic abuse, and that's all." Her words trailed off.

González heard someone murmur in the background. A woman's voice urged her to continue.

He asked her again about the axe.

"It wasn't no axe. It was just the head, it didn't have no handle, ya know what I mean?"

* * *

Pauline walked into the courthouse in the same dress she had worn when she met González. She was drunk, disheveled and smelled like sour wine—vomited wine, thought González when he talked to her in the hallway.

"I'm going to fight this one. You with me?"

She leaned on González for support. He held his breath to keep from gagging.

"You don't have a chance. The judge is going to tell you to move and he'll give you forty-eight hours."

"I want my money then. They owe me fifty bucks, and they cut my cord. I want the money for that."

"You'll be lucky if you walk away from this without owing Donley a couple hundred dollars."

Lines of worry creased her forehead. She did not want to owe anybody any money. She had no idea what would happen if the judge said she had to pay Donley and she did not want to learn.

"What can I do then?"

"How much time do you need to move?"

"Jeez, I don't have no money, and I don't know when Joey's gettin' out. I don't even have a place yet. Two weeks, at least two weeks."

"I'll get you a week. But if you don't leave, Donley can have the sheriff out there to move your stuff, you understand?"

"Sure." She paused for a few seconds. "I can do that. A week. No sweat."

González had to sell the idea to Donley.

Rose was ready to testify and Donley had memorized his arguments. He wanted his court costs, the rent for March and something for cleaning up after Pauline and Joey.

"Look around you, Donley. The courtroom is packed. Judge Kerso is still on the 8:30 returns and it's already 9:45. He's up there giving lawyers hell for not knowing their cases should have been assigned to Courtroom 9-H. He's only warming up. It will be 11:00 by the time he gets to us. And sure, he's going to tell Pauline and Joey to move their junk, but I'm going to convince him that you rented a place that doesn't meet the

Housing Code. He's likely to order the Health Department out to your place just so they can close you up for a while."

"González, you must think I'm an idiot. You know he can't do that. He's not on the Code Enforcement docket anymore."

"No, but he sure as hell would rather be there than in this courtroom listening to all this bullshit. His old habits are going to take time to break, Donley. You know we're going to be here until this afternoon, which means a simple eviction will throw off his whole docket today. He won't like that, especially when I let him know we were willing to move out if you hadn't been so stubborn about trying to get some money out of these people. You ever hear about blood out of a turnip?"

Donley agreed to give Pauline a week.

On the way out of the courthouse Pauline touched González's arm and told him thanks. He could not shake the feeling that he had missed something.

The next day started badly for González. His beat-up van gave out on him on the Speer Boulevard viaduct. He backed up traffic for two miles before he found the loose ignition wire and managed to tighten it enough to make it to the office.

The uneasiness that started during Pauline's case returned. He felt on the edge.

The receptionist chewed him out for not telling her he would be late. He grunted and picked up a dozen telephone messages form his mail slot, all marked "urgent." His desk was stacked with intake sheets, all marked "urgent." Case files littered the floor, the bookcases and the tops of filing cabinets.

He loosened his tie, shut the door and turned on his radio. Music from The Blasters asked him if he was going to have a time tonight. He nodded his head to the beat as he waited for calls from clients stuck in crap up to their elbows. They would continue almost nonstop until lunch when González escaped for some green chile and a beer at Joe's Buffet on Santa Fe.

That afternoon the chile churned angrily in the pit of his stomach when his secretary told him Crazy Chuck was in the waiting room. Chuck wanted to talk about a few problems at the projects.

Charles Luévano was a big, muscular Chicano in his late forties who had spent more time in prison than his age would allow, or so he said. González had seen his record and he was amazed at the list of burglaries, hold-ups, assaults, drug busts and bad checks. How many crimes can one man commit in one life? González guessed that Chuck was free because he was stone crazy, *loco*, "a few problems with my head." You had to be a little insane to survive on the streets.

Chuck loved to talk. He could go on for hours about things that made no sense but that, according to Chuck, required the immediate filing of a complaint in federal court because his "civil and due process rights were abridged, man."

González stared at the hulking, fidgety man. Chuck had salt and pepper hair brushed straight back from his forehead. The rolled-up sleeves of his blue work shirt revealed tattooed roses, initials, crosses and a leaping black panther.

The uneasiness had turned into a pounding knot lodged in the middle of the lawyer's forehead.

"*Mira, ese*. I got to have something done, m-a-a-an. Those white devils in the housing are going to spray my place for cockroaches, and I ain't got none, man. That spray only kills me. It don't do nothin' to those bugs. They been around for a million years. What do those honkies know about killin' those bugs? My system won't put up with that stuff, man. I'm allergic to that spray, it screws up my lungs, makes me cough. Shit, man, that shit will kill me before any of those goddamned roaches kick. They just sprayed last year and what happened? Not a goddamned thing, except to me, man. I'm disabled, a ward of the government, they can't do this to me. They know how bad I am. I got a bullet in my gut." He lifted his shirt and showed González the scar. "And they want to spray with some poison that will just jack me up, m-a-a-an."

His words came out in a slow, sinusy whine.

"You know me, man, I'm an old *tecato*. I seen it all and the *chotas* know it. They're out to get me for years. They got snitches all over the projects, watching me, trying to get me to do some really funny shit. Out of nowhere, they come up to me and try to sell me shit man, shit like I ain't seen for years, shit that even the goddamned mayor can't get, and they want to sell it to *me*, man, me." He thumped his chest with the palm of his hand and González jumped at the hollow sound. "Why, *ese*, why to me all of a sudden? Because they got me labeled a career criminal. Shit, I ain't no career criminal, man. I ain't got no money like a career criminal should have. If I did would I be talkin' to legal aid? Hell no. I'd be talkin' to some fancy defense lawyer, but my jacket says career criminal, m-a-a-an."

González needed help. The bad feeling had festered and burst into a melancholy hysteria. He saw drunken Pauline standing shakily in the courthouse hall, leaning on him, grabbing at his coat, thanking him with words that reached into his throat and gagged him.

An odor of a thousand other clients mixed with that of Pauline and Chuck filled his nostrils. He smelled despair, fear, weakness. He was suffocating. His fingers scratched for fresh air.

Chuck rambled on about white devils and cockroaches.

Sweat popped out on the skin beneath the lawyer's moustache. He started to laugh; tears rolled down his face.

He stood up.

Chuck stopped in mid-sentence, open-mouthed, outcrazied by his own lawyer.

González watched himself grab the larger man by the head and ram his face into the wall. Blood spurted from the skull and flowed onto yellow sheets of paper and manila folders. Chuck slumped to the floor and González was free.

He ran out of the office and into the coffee room. His hands shook as he poured a cup of the day-old, bitter liquid. He took a long drink. He talked to himself to try to gain control. His breath escaped in heavy, rushing surges, and chills crawled up his spine.

González knew he would go back to his dreary office and listen to Crazy Chuck for as long as the man could talk and at the end he would treat him like a real client, offer advice on dealing with the killer cockroach spray and shake his hand goodbye. And he would do the same for the client after Chuck, for the next Pauline and for all the others.

González made a living representing crazies, weirdos, misfits, losers and plain folks who got taken. Sometimes it was hard to distinguish between client and lawyer, sanity and craziness. But each morning he reminded himself he was not a burned out liberal who took up space on legal aid's payroll. He was an ace attorney for the underdog.

WHEN PIGS FLY AND MONKEYS TALK

Black lightening twisted across the red sky. "Winter," Cantú mumbled. She thumped the control panel and Sanitex snapped over the porthole.

She tightened her tunic as though the silver crystals had already started to fall. The rigo skin deflected moisture but it was useless for warmth.

"What do I expect from a flying pig?"

She trudged around the accumulated junk spread throughout the Shak3. Pumps and pipe sections blocked the rear exit. Somewhere in the clutter a sand monkey huddled among discarded circuit boards. The smelly thing treasured scrap as food. Cantú appreciated that it had quit screeching and jabbering at her.

The portable shelter trembled. Cantú twitched when she heard the high-pitched whine.

She tapped Latif's numbers on her digi-tel. Her partner's hairy face glowed from the small screen.

"What the hell you doin' out there? Can't you feel that wind?"

Latif's voice cracked through Cantú's headphones. "I'm trying to get back. If you haven't noticed, it's a little tough moving around this goddamned planet. The Oscar is stuck in some kind of mush and I don't really want to walk in the open. I'm waiting out the wind in a crag hole. I'm not that far away."

"What do you mean, waiting out? This could go on for weeks. What about the wind snakes? You want to hassle with those?"

The screen blinked, then faded to gray. Either Latif had hung up or the wind had cut off access, again.

What a nightmare assignment. Coughing fits from the acrid, metallic atmosphere that lasted for hours; weird, hungry creatures; and a climate fit only for rocks and gray scrub. But there was oil—at least something that might be used as oil. The lab boys called it Synth, short for synthetic, she figured, but it floated naturally on the puddles of smoking liquid that dotted the otherwise barren landscape. She and Latif had been told to never touch the stuff—the standard bureaucratic caution. No one knew what Synth was, but that didn't matter to corporate. The potential payoff canceled any concern about the actual risks. If the wages weren't so good, she would have quit a long time ago.

Latif's shriek wrenched her eyes from the blank digi-tel. Her co-worker stumbled into the Shak3. Synth clung to Latif like a mercurial cocoon.

"I fell . . . I can't breathe." Latif clawed at his own chest.

Cantú recoiled when Latif burst into flames. The wind swallowed her scream. The burning man collapsed at Cantú's feet. A trickle of blue flowed from the crackling corpse. The thin stream moved towards Cantú. She turned to run but a slimy chord grabbed her ankle. The sinewy fluid latched onto her legs and crawled up to her mouth. It forced her teeth open, sliced her tongue. Oil filled her throat.

A small, furry face peered from under a pile of useless computers. The sand monkey watched Cantú burn.

"I tried to warn them," the ambassador later reported. "It's not my fault."

OUTLAWS

THE SKULL OF PANCHO VILLA

You've heard the story, maybe read something about it in the newspaper or a magazine. How Pancho Villa's grave was robbed in 1926 and his head taken. Emil Homdahl, a mercenary and pre-CIA spy, what they used to call a soldier of fortune, is usually "credited" with the theft. He was arrested in Mexico but quickly released because of lack of evidence—some say because of political pressure from north of the border. Eventually, the story goes, he sold his trophy to Prescott Bush, grandfather of you-know-who. And now the skull is stashed at a fancy college back East. The story has legs, as they say. There are websites about Pancho and his missing skull, and I heard about a recent book that runs with the legend, featuring Homdahl, a mystery writer, and a bag full of skulls, all the way to a bloody shoot-out ending. Haven't read it, so don't know for sure.

That's all bull, of course. Oh yeah, Villa's corpse is minus a skull but Homdahl never had it, the poor sap. The thing is that everyone overlooks one detail. There was another guy arrested with Homdahl, a Chicano from Los Angeles by the name of Alberto Corral. I'm serious—you can look it up. He was quickly released, too, and then he disappeared off the historical page, unlike Homdahl, who apparently liked the attention and actually enjoyed his grave-robbing notoriety. Corral's role in the tale is given short shrift, something we Chicanos understand all too well. If he's remembered at all, it's as Homdahl's flunky, the muscle who dug up the grave or broke into the tomb, depending on the version of the story, and who was paid with a few pesos and a bottle of tequila while the gringo made twenty-five grand off old man Bush.

Yeah, I know what you're thinking. Gus Corral is off on another wild hair, this time about his great-grandfather. And I could do that, easy. But that's not it. Whatever happened eighty years ago, happened. I don't know why Grandpa Alberto ended up with the skull and I don't care. No one ever told me how he was connected to Homdahl or whatever possessed him to want to steal Pancho's head, and I don't expect to find out. All I know is that the skull has been taken care of by the Corral family for as long as I can remember. Wrapped in old rags and then plastic bags and stored in various containers like hatboxes, cardboard chests and even a see-through case designed for a basketball, you know, for sports collectors. Whispered about by the kids who caught glimpses of the creepy yellowish thing whenever the adults dragged it out, usually on the nights when the tequila and beer and whiskey flowed long and strong.

My grandmother Otilia sang to it, the "Corrido de Pancho Villa," of course. The tiny, dark old woman, hunched under a shawl and often with a red bandana wrapped around her gray, fine hair, drank slowly from a glass of whiskey while she stared at the box that held Panchito, that's what she called it, for several minutes, and meanwhile all the kids waited for what we knew was coming. And then, without warning, Otilia would rip off the box, grab the skull, expose it to the light, and simultaneously burst into weepy lyrics about the Robin Hood of Mexico. One of my uncles, also into his cups, would join in by strumming loudly on an old guitar. Shouts and whoops and *ay-yi-yis* erupted from whoever else was in the house and the little kids would scatter from the room, shrieking and crying, while us older ones were hypnotized by the dark eye sockets and crooked teeth of the skull of Pancho Villa.

You can imagine what a jolt it was when the skull was stolen from my sister's house.

Corrine—she's the oldest, and the flakiest—called me one night, around midnight. Not all that unusual, if you know Corrine. One crisis after another, I swear. One of her boys (they all got brats of their own but Corrine still calls them her boys) needs to get bailed out and do I have about five hundred dollars? Or she slipped and banged up her knee and can't walk or drive and can I pick her up for bingo? Or the latest love of her sad life went out for a six-pack and hasn't come back, about a week ago, and could I go look for him?

I knew she shouldn't have the skull but she is the oldest and when only the three of us remained—my younger sister, Maxine, is cute and naïve (I didn't say stupid) but that's another story—Corrine claimed rights to the skull and took it out of our parents' house before Max or I knew what was happening. Which was ironic. Corrine always said she hated that "disgusting *cosa*." But there she was, all over Panchito like he was gold. I kind of understood. Panchito was one of the few things our parents left us and just about the only connection we had to the old-timers of the family.

Anyway, Corrine is totally unreliable—maybe you picked up on that? I'm not perfect, no way, but at least I got a job managing my ex-wife's *segunda* over on Thirty-second. Six days a week, from opening at nine in the morning until Sylvia, the ex, shows up around two in the afternoon. I'm also the night watchman, which means I sleep in the place so I don't have to worry about rent as long as I don't go back to the store until Sylvia leaves. Sylvia provides a cot but she won't say more than two words to me even when she digs into the cash register and calculates my weekly pay. We both like it like that.

I argued with Corrine about Panchito. I pointed out that the parade of losers that camped out at her house were a major security risk. I added that I could keep the skull at Sylvia's shop. It fit in with the musty junk Sylvia thinks are antiques, but she clutched that skull like a baby and it was clear that the only way I would get my hands on it was to rip it from hers, which I wasn't going to even attempt. Corrine has like fifty pounds on me.

She had Panchito for about a year, and I hadn't thought about it. The call woke me from a mixed-up dream. I crawled off my cot and answered the shop's phone.

"You got your nerve, Gus!" she shouted over the line. "I can't believe you took it. What'd you do, pawn it for beer money?"

"What the hell are you screaming about? It's midnight, in case you didn't know."

I'm not quick with the comebacks with Corrine. She's always intimidated me that way, since we were kids.

"Panchito! Panchito!"

As if that explained everything.

A half hour later I had the story and she started to believe that I hadn't broken into her house and stolen the skull. She had come home from an evening with the girls—right—and found the back door wide open and a pair of her panties on the lawn. She freaked immediately and called the cops. She waited outside, not chancing that the intruder might still be inside. When the cops gave her the all-clear, she entered a house torn upside down and inside out. Her clothes were scattered everywhere, drawers were ripped from dressers, bowls of food dripped on the kitchen floor and a trail of CD cases snaked from her CD player to the useless back door. The final straw made her hysterical. A large wet stain of piss sat in the middle of her carpet.

Did she think I was really capable of that? I could see how she might be suspicious of me concerning the skull, but to trash her place and pee on her rug? Please.

The cops said that they couldn't find any evidence of a forced entry so they concluded that Corrine left the back door open and one of the neighborhood kids probably saw it from the alley. A crime of opportunity, they told her. I can see her face when she heard that. She must have screamed that she was absolutely sure she had locked the door and then most likely she turned into a blubbery mess, but she was just covering. Corrine often forgot to lock up. Attention to detail never was one of her strong points. One time she came home and found a pot of beans completely black, the beans nothing more than a congealed mass, and smoke as thick as her chubby arms filling every room. A fire truck pulled up a few minutes later. It was months before the drapes and walls didn't smell like burned beans. She told me she couldn't remember doing anything with beans, much less leaving the stove on. A classic bit of Corrine.

I had to agree with the cops. The way Corrine's house was wrecked and the stuff that was taken—CDs, video tapes, a jar full of pennies and a bag of potato chips—sounded like a kid's thing. But what the hell would he do with a skull?

Corrine never mentioned Panchito to the cops. She told me that she had it in a Styrofoam cooler at the back of her coat closet near the front door. The cooler was still in the closet, empty. The coats had been tossed on the front room couch, and she guessed that the thief had taken the skull in one of the pillowcases missing from her bed. The cops said that was a tried-and-true method for burglars to haul away their booty, in the vic's own pillowcases or trash bags.

I knew that the cops would never arrest anyone. We got so many unsolved break-ins on the North Side that the police will give you a number to use when you call in to ask about your case—they don't need your name or address, just your number. It's been that way for years, but the new mayor has promised to do something about the North Side crime rate, which means that City Hall is finally noticing all the young white couples with two big dogs and one little blond-haired rug rat that have been moving into the neighborhood. Sylvia calls them yuppies, but I don't think anyone uses that term anymore, except Sylvia, I guess.

The next day after work I started asking around but I couldn't say too much, you know. The Corral family hadn't exactly been up front about Panchito. We had assumed that possession of Pancho's skull was illegal and the desecration of the grave of a Mexican hero certainly wouldn't do anything for the family reputation. Mexico could demand Panchito's return and the U.S. government could back away from us and might declare that we were as illegal as the skull and deport us, although Corrine, Max and I hadn't set foot in Mexico since we were infants, a trip we couldn't even remember. So for two days I asked about any kids who had been trying to get rid of CDs that didn't seem right for them—Tony Bennett, Frank Sinatra, Miguel Aceves Mejía—and a jar of pennies. It was ridiculous but what else is new in my life?

I asked old friends who still called me "bro"; I quizzed waitresses at a couple of Mexican restaurants. My questions made more than one pool player nervous; and the ballers that crowded the court at Chaffee Park swore they didn't know *nada*. Those NBA wannabes wouldn't tell me anything anyway.

On the second day my search took me to the beer joints. It had to happen.

I got nothing from the barflies, naturally. They scowled like I had asked for money, never a popular question in any bar I'd ever been in, and a couple of the souses didn't even look at me when I spoke to them. I decided to take a break. Detective work had made me thirsty, and the Holiday Bar and Grill always had very cold beer, but there wasn't a grill in sight.

Accordion music blared in the background and a pair of muscular women wearing their boyfriends' colors played eight ball along a side wall. There were a couple of other guys at the bar, and the three of us were entertained by Jackie, the bartender who worked the afternoon-early evening shift at the Holiday.

Jackie methodically wiped a glass with a bright yellow bar rag and blinked her inch-long eyelashes at me. I worried for a hot sec that the weight of what looked like caterpillars sitting on her eyelids might permanently shut Jackie O's eyes, but it didn't seem to be a problem. Jackie O—that's what she wanted to be called, but I remembered when she was just plain old Javier Ortega, which, as you might guess, is another story entirely. I hardly ever used the O in her name; I just couldn't bring myself to say it. I had to comment about her outfit and headdress.

"Trying for the Carmen Miranda look today, Jackie?"

"Don't be foolish. These are just a few old things I had around the house. A summer adventure. You like?" She twirled and clapped her hands, kind of in flamenco style. The two guys down the bar gagged on their beer. I kept a straight face.

"Nice. That shade is good on you."

"What you been up to, Gus? I don't see you in here too much anymore."

"Same old, you know how it is." She nodded. "But Corrine got ripped off the other night, maybe you heard about it? They broke in her house and took a couple thousand dollars worth of stuff. At least that's what she told the insurance. Too much, huh? I'm trying to find out who would do such a thing, maybe get some of Corrine's stuff back. Maybe kick some ass." I threw that last part in but I knew she knew it was just talk.

She almost dropped the glass. She turned away quickly and helped the two guys who couldn't seem to get enough of her show. I picked up a bad vibe off Jackie and it bothered me. We went back a long ways and I recognized her signals. I sipped on my beer and out of the corner of my eye I could see her looking at me through her heavily accessorized lashes. Again, I felt foolish. This was not like Jackie.

She reached under the bar and pulled out a bottle of what I was drinking. She opened it and brought it to me, although I hadn't ordered another.

"Let's have a smoke, Gus. I need one bad."

Now we had moved into strange. For one thing, Jackie knew I didn't smoke. For another, although the recent anti-smoking ordinance meant that all smoking had to be done outside the premises, I couldn't remember when that particular law had ever been enforced in the Holiday, especially during the afternoon-early evening shift when there wasn't anyone in the bar, to speak of.

But I went with it. She snapped her fingers at the women playing pool. "I'll be right back, Lori," she shouted. "Come get me if anyone comes in."

One of the women shouted back, "Whatever."

I followed Jackie's sashaying hips into the alley.

She lit a smoke and dragged on it nervously. I waited. Like most of the women in my life, Sylvia being the prime example, Jackie loved drama. Jackie could emote, that's for sure.

When she finished sucking the life out of half the smoke, she whispered, "I shouldn't say anything. But we been friends forever, Gus. You backed me up when I needed it. You can't ever let on that you got this from me. I'll call you a damn liar. I mean it, Gus. You swear, on your mother's grave, Gus? On your mother's grave."

See what I mean.

Her face was lost in the twilight and the glowing tip of her cigarette didn't give off enough light for me to see how serious she was, so I took her at her word.

"Okay, Jackie. I swear. I never heard nothing from you. Which so far is the truth."

"Jessie Salazar was in last night."

I heard that name and I wanted a cigarette.

"I thought he was in the pen," I said. "Limon or Cañon City. Supermax."

"He was. Did five years, but he was here last night. I had to fill in for Artie, he got sick or something or I wouldn't even know Salazar was around. He showed up with his old crew. All dressed up in a suit, smelling like Macy's perfume counter. Talking loud and stupid. Same old crazy Jessie. He said things about your family, and you. That chicken-shit stuff between the Corrals and the Salazars. He said the great payback had begun, that's what he called it, but that there was more hell to pay. He talks like that, remember?"

I felt like someone punched my gut. I couldn't say anything.

"He never got over that Corrine testified against him," Jackie continued. "I didn't think anything about it last night. That happens in here all the time. Guys blow off steam, then the next day forget all about it. More so if the guy just got out of the joint. But when you said someone had broken into Corrine's house, I got to thinking. Salazar's that kind of punk. He could have trashed Corrine's house, easy, but if he did, that's just the beginning. You got to tell her, and you got to watch your back, Gus. He always thought you should have stopped her, controlled Corrine. He blames you for him doing time."

Jackie stomped on her cigarette. I smiled weakly and walked away through the alley. I stopped and turned and waved at Jackie. "Thanks," I said.

"*Cuídate*, Gus," Jackie said. "Be careful."

Crazy Jessie had been my number one life problem for most of my life. He was the school bully, then the neighborhood gangster and eventually he passed through reform school and the state penitentiary. I tangled with him several times when we were younger. My mother and his mother had been rivals when they were low-riding North Side cholas, and I had heard many stories about parties gone bad, fights on school yards and in nightclubs. That nonsense just kept on when they had their own kids. Corrine and I often brushed up against Jessie and his brothers and sisters, not always coming out on top. But we held our own.

Corrine was having dinner one night about six years ago with the latest love of her sad life when Jessie stormed into La Cocina restaurant waving a handgun. He terrorized the customers, pistol-whipped the owner and took cash, wallets, purses and jewelry. That happened when Jessie was strung out bad on his drug of choice at that time. Corrine talked to the cops and fingered Jessie without hesitation, but her date denied recognizing the gunman. Hell, he wasn't sure that there had even been a disturbance, if you know what I mean. Didn't matter to Corrine. She gave Jessie to the cops and testified in court. I was proud of her but also a little bit nervous. We all relaxed when they turned Jessie over to the Department of Corrections. We thought he would be gone for a very long time. Five years didn't seem long enough, but then I never understood the so-called justice system.

I knew where to find Jessie. I just didn't know if I wanted to find him. I had to warn Corrine, and I gave serious consideration to forgetting about Panchito. I thought that the thug might leave us alone now that he had vented on Corrine's property and he had the skull. I could see him shaking his head about his discovery in Corrine's closet, thinking that the Corrals were way weirder than he had always assumed.

I tried to call Corrine on my cheap cell phone but the service was weak on the North Side, which meant it didn't do much for me. I got a busy signal, but that wasn't right. I should have gone to her voice mail.

Jessie's crib was in the opposite direction from Corrine. He had a small house on a hill that overlooked the interstate, right on the edge of the North Side where all the new condos were going up. Yuppie hell, Sylvia called it. The house had been the Salazar home forever and it had always been a dump. But with the wave of newcomers and the frenzy of construction, the shack must have doubled or tripled in value since Jessie had been sent away, although Jessie would never know what to do with that piece of information. One of his deadbeat sisters technically owned the place, but as sure as I knew that Jessie's urine had stained my sister's carpet, I also knew that he was living in that house.

Okay, right about now you're thinking, call the cops, Gus. Don't be a *pendejo*. Let the law handle it. But see, you don't live in my world, man. Where I come from, the cops aren't your first line of defense. You didn't grow up constantly squaring off against *cabrones* like Jessie. You never had to accept that every lousy week another clown would challenge your manhood and you would have to beat or be beaten. You never had to explain to your old man why your sister came home in tears and you didn't do a damn thing about the bastard who slapped her around. You never sat in a cell in the City Jail staring down the ugly face of what your life could become if you didn't do the right thing.

I had to stop for gas and I used the restroom at the 7-Eleven. Stalling, for sure. It took me a while to make it to Jessie's, but eventually I was there.

I parked about a block away and did my best to be inconspicuous. Construction equipment was everywhere, and a few of the projects had crews working late, overtime. Steel beams stretched to the sky and white concrete slabs waited. I had played ball in these lots, had made out with girls and drank beer with my pals. No one who ever lived in the new buildings would know that or care about those things.

I made my way up the alley behind Jessie's house. I picked up a piece of rebar, two feet long, not thinking about how inadequate it was for the job I had to do. The night had a gray tint from the construction lights. Rap music blared from his back yard. I crawled behind a dumpster and peeked through the chain-link fence.

Jessie was sprawled on the dirt, an ugly hole in his head leaked blood and a messy soup of other stuff.

The guy standing over the body, holding a gun, looked like a junior version of Jessie, except he was alive. Another worthless gangbanger, extracting his own revenge for whatever Jessie might have inflicted, maybe in that back yard that evening, maybe in a jail cell that was too small for the both of them, maybe years ago for something that Jessie couldn't remember.

I guess no one had heard the shot. The construction could have drowned it or the rap music might have covered up the crime. And sometimes gunshots have no sound on the North Side.

The guy spit on Jessie. He tucked the gun in the back waist of his pants and jumped over the fence. I inched closer to the dumpster and my luck held. He walked the other way, whistling, if I remember right.

I swung open the gate and tried to sneak into the back yard. No one else was in the house. Whoever had capped Jessie would have made sure of that. I looked all over that yard, except at the oozing body at my feet.

Panchito perched on a concrete block. A lime green sombrero with red dingle balls balanced on his slick, shiny head, and an unlit, droopy cigar dangled from his mouth hole. I was embarrassed for him. I removed the hat and cigar and picked him up. There was a dirty pillowcase on the ground. I wrapped Panchito in it.

It was a long walk back to my car and a long drive to Corrine's. I never heard any sirens, and no one stopped me. I drove in silence thinking about what had happened, trying to piece together coincidence and luck. I never thought so hard in my life.

My luck had been amazing and I toyed with the idea of going back to the 7-Eleven for a lottery ticket. But I wasn't the lucky type. Had never won anything in my life. I thought even harder about what had happened.

Corrine opened the door slowly. She let me in but didn't say anything. I set the bundle on her kitchen table.

She smiled.

"How'd you find out about Jessie? Who was that guy?" I blurted out my questions as quickly as I could. I didn't want to give her time to make up something.

"You're the smart one. Figure it out yourself."

"Jackie. She called you, told you what she had told me. Said I was probably going over to Jessie's."

"Close. She said you were on your way to get killed by that son-of-a-bitch."

"And the guy? What's that all about?"

"You remember him. Charley Maestas. He lived here about six months, a while back. Too young for me, turned out. He owed Jessie for a lot of grief, something awful about his sister, but he had to wait for Jessie to do his time. I let Charley know that Jessie was out and where he could find him, and the rest was up to him. I said Jessie was getting ready to book so he had to deal with him tonight. I thought the least he could do was give you some help if you got over your head. I guess Charley took care of the whole thing?" She asked but she didn't really want an answer.

I shrugged. It turned out to be simple. Corrine and one of the loves of her sad life. North Side justice often is simple. Direct, bloody and simple.

My older sister picked up Panchito and gave him a quick wipe with the pillowcase. She carried him to the closet, dug out the cooler, placed the skull in it and shut the door.

As I walked out the back I hollered, "I like the new rug!"

IF WE HAD BEEN DANCING

I walked into the bar the same as I had a hundred times before and my thoughts were the same as a hundred times before.

This is all I have to do after work? Drink beer, shoot the bull with the bar flies, flirt with Maggie, throw a dollar in the jukebox? What a life.

Maggie winked and popped open a beer before I had made it to my stool. She slid it in front of me and said, "How's it hangin', Álvarez? Workin' hard or hardly workin'?"

She laughed, the boys two stools over laughed and I grinned a little. That's what she always said and it bugged me, but that's what happened at the Club Lido. A man had to put up with Maggie's clichés if he wanted to drink cold Bud in a bottle for two bucks.

In the background a one-hit wonder soul singer cried about his ba-a-a-by breaking his poor ole li'l heart and the boys two stools over told lawyer jokes.

I had nothing but respect for Maggie. She had grown up in the neighborhood around the bar and spent so much time in the Club Lido that when she started tending the bar no one thought much about it. Seemed like a natural place for her.

I peeled off my damp jacket and draped it over the stool next to me, then swept my hand through my hair to shake out some of the raindrops that hadn't yet run down the back of my neck. My sweater was wet, too, but I needed to keep that on. I sucked down half of the brew before I looked around the place. Same old dirty windows looking out on the same old rain-slicked street, same old grimy pool table, same old tired face staring back at me from the stained and cracked mirror behind the bar. Nothing had changed.

The door to the bar opened, letting in cold, moist air, but I ignored it and concentrated on my beer.

That's when the girl picked up my jacket and eased herself onto the stool next to me. My beer stopped halfway to my mouth.

She said, "This yours?"

I took it from her hand and dropped it between the bar rail and the floor. It was an old jacket without any sentimental value, and I wanted to look at her and not the jacket. She had a small, pinched face with a thin nose and thin lips that held a droopy cigarette. Black, very short hair hung across her forehead and dripped wetly down her neck. She looked like a duckling who had been thrown in the lake by the mama duck before she knew how to tread water. She wore jeans, boots, a loose red scarf, a black T-shirt and a denim vest that exposed skinny arms and a three-inch tattoo of Our Lady of Guadalupe crushing a snake with her bare foot. And when she looked at me she did it with a pair of brown eyes that were tinged with the gray smoke of her cigarette and the cobalt shadow of her soggy hair.

Maggie turned to her and asked, "What'll you have, honey?"

The girl smiled, at the word honey, I assumed, and said, "Jack, black. Plenty of ice."

She stubbed out her wet smoke and plucked another one from a wrinkled pack she had dragged out of a bulky red leather purse that hung on her hip, the strap twisted across her narrow shoulders. She seemed to move to the beat of the music.

So I asked, "You like this song?"

She finished lighting her cigarette, carefully put the match in the ashtray, filled her lungs with smoke, let it all go in a big cloud of drama. She tapped the bar, then she turned to me.

"Yeah, I do as a matter of fact. Something about this song that makes me feel like a teenager again, know what I mean? A teenager getting ready for the prom, thinking that she's about to lose her cherry, maybe. Know what I mean?"

It was my turn to take my time. I drank my beer, picked at the label with my fingernail and then looked into the crazy house of those eyes. I said, "I never thought of it that way, actually. It's more like this bittersweet poem about a man's foolishness and the price he pays for being a man."

She licked the wet edge of her glass with a tiny pink tongue and did a move with her shoulders that could have been a dance step, if we had been on the dance floor, if we had been dancing. When she finished with the motions, she said, "A foolish man. It's always a foolish man."

Right then I knew that our dance had finished before it had even started. She had to be under the weight of a story that was guaranteed to bore me or make me laugh or maybe even make me feel pity for her, but none of those responses was what she wanted. The truth of the matter was that I would never figure out what she was looking for, not if we had all the time in the world to sit in that bar and talk about it. Not if we went to her place and spent the night talking about it, not even if she told me all about it while we lay naked in her bed, smoking cigarettes. I would never know because what she carried around with her was not for me to know. It's a lesson I had learned in that bar so long ago that I had forgotten my teacher but I had never forgotten the lesson.

I shrugged and let it go. Maybe she wanted to get picked up. Maybe she only wanted a drink. Maybe she was waiting for the latest in a long line of foolish men, and maybe he was the kind of guy who would not appreciate another man talking to her about the implications of the sensual vocalizing streaming from the jukebox. It got all complicated right then and there and I decided that I should have another beer. I waved my empty bottle at Maggie and she retrieved one from the cooler at the end of the bar. Almost simultaneously, the girl hollered, "Hey, another Jack, black. More ice."

One of the boys next to her said, "Put that on my tab, Maggie. Let me buy the little lady a drink."

I winced and waited for something, anything, because what the guy said just didn't seem right and a response of some kind had to be on its way.

The girl said, "Hey, I never pass up a free drink. Thanks, mister."

Then she turned to me.

"Your friends okay? Or are they maybe perverts who want to get me drunk and do something really nasty to a little thing like me?"

The boys laughed and she laughed and I laughed and I thought that at any minute the Club Lido would turn weird. But it was weird in that bar all the time, and I told myself that whatever I was watching had nothing to do with me.

I kept an eye on Maggie, who had proven to be a good gauge for weirdness and trouble. When something was about to break, she could sense it. Fifteen years of serving drinks to crowds of men in varying stages of inebriation will do that. She often had a bat in her hand at the same instant that a drunk decided to trash the place, and then he would either leave or she would open up his forehead with the bat. I had seen it and I trusted her to figure out the girl.

Maggie did not offer any body language that told me anything about the girl. She served us our drinks and I tried to relax and enjoy my rest stop after work.

One of the boys said, "Hey now, that ain't us, sweetheart. Ask Maggie there. She'll vouch for us. We're okay. Right, Maggie?"

The bartender had her head back in the cooler, counting beer bottles, so none of us could see her face when she said, "A couple of teddy bears, honey. Real gentlemen. Just don't believe them when they say they want you to meet their mother."

The boys laughed again, a bit nervously I thought.

The girl stood up from her stool and moved a little behind us. She had her hand in her purse. I offered her a cigarette from a pack I had sitting on the bar, but she shook her head and persisted in digging in that purse. The boys went back to telling jokes because it looked as if the girl would play with that purse for a long time.

I had to make a decision. A glass of bourbon meant that it could turn into a longer night than I had anticipated at the Club Lido. I could leave now, grab a burger on the way home and get a good night of sleep. A loud clap of thunder shook the outside world and the lights in the bar flickered. Rain fell in sheets against the dirty windows and I no longer had to make a decision. There was no way I would run to my car in the downpour.

I tried to get Maggie's attention, but she stared only at the girl, still standing behind us. Maggie looked sick, and I worried that maybe she had eaten too many of the microwave burritos that were Club Lido's specialty.

Maggie said, "Hey, honey, put that away. There's no need for that."

I turned and saw a very shiny handgun pointed in the general direction of Maggie but whose sweep had to include me and the boys two stools over.

I said, "Damn."

The boys stopped talking and one of them raised his hands above his head. He apparently had some experience with the situation, and so his buddy and I followed his lead.

Maggie said, "Honey, put that away. I mean it. This is stupid. There's no need."

The girl waved the gun at Maggie, and Maggie stopped talking. The girl had not said a word for several minutes but she communicated very well, I thought.

She kept the gun pointed at all of us while she moved in the general direction of Maggie. She walked behind the bar, sneered at the two boys with their hands in the air, then rested the barrel of her gun against Maggie's temple.

Her words came out in a whisper and I almost didn't believe what I heard her say.

"*Cabrona.* I told you not to mess with me. Here I am, Maggie, just like I promised."

The boys looked at each other, then at Maggie, then at me. I raised my eyebrows at them, although I didn't understand what I meant by that.

Maggie rotated her neck as if she were warming up for an exercise class. A tear slowly made its way down her cheek, leaving a trail through the make-up that she wore with pride. She said, "Honey, we can talk this out. What you think you're doing? Put that gun away and let's go home and talk about this. This is crazy, honey. Crazy."

The girl pressed the gun into Maggie's head, and Maggie quit rotating her neck.

"*¡Cabrona! ¡Cabrona, cabrona!* I *told* you not to mess with me. You can't dump me, *vieja. Vieja cabrona.* You can't dump me!"

Tears from those wild eyes raced down her face and her thin lips quivered. I feared that her shaking might cause her to pull the trigger by accident.

One of the boys said, "What the hell is this? What's this dyke to you, Maggie?"

The girl pointed the gun at the boy, and he shut up, but it was too late. The shot sounded like a blast from a cannon. He twirled on his bar stool and flew across space until he landed on his back on the muddy floor.

He said, "Oh God. She shot me. She shot me."

His right hand gripped his left shoulder where blood oozed across his fingers. His friend's wide-open eyes gaped at the blood. Large tears formed at the corners of those eyes. There seemed to be a lot of crying, and I was starting to feel a little emotional myself.

Maggie said, "Oh, hell, Diana, you've done it now. You plan to shoot all of us? Kill me and these guys just because you can't take it that it's over between us? You are crazy. I knew it and now you've proven it."

I didn't like the fact that Maggie appeared to be giving ideas to the girl about what she had to do next, but I didn't want to say anything. The last person who had intruded into what was obviously a lovers' spat had ended up whimpering on the floor while a pool of his blood slowly radiated around his upper torso. I did not want to join him.

The girl finally spoke.

"I don't care about you, bitch. You think that's what this is about? You give yourself too much credit, hag. I want the money. Clean out the cash drawer and get the stuff from the back, in the safe. Then I'm out of here, and you and your *puta* can live happily ever after, for all I care."

Maggie shook her head as if she wanted to take the girl in her arms and soothe the bad feelings.

The girl screamed, "Do it! Get the *pinche* money! Get it now!"

She waved the gun in the air with herky-jerky spasms of her hands. I bobbed and weaved like a punch-drunk palooka to keep out of the line that a stray bullet might travel.

Maggie continued shaking her head, not ready to believe what was happening, but she opened the cash register drawer and scooped out a wad of bills. She was handing them over to the girl when the siren froze everyone. The money hung in midair between Maggie and the girl. The wounded boy did not groan, did not twist in his blood. His friend did not shake. And I did not lick my lips, although my thirst had become a cotton football stuck in my throat since I had decided that I would stop at Club Lido for a couple of beers after work.

Maggie said, "Someone heard the shot. Called the cops. Now what?"

The girl looked stupidly at Maggie. She hesitated, but the siren got louder and she finally understood she had to do something. The money was forgotten. She hugged Maggie, the gun resting on Maggie's shoulder, and gave her a kiss that seemed too long under the circumstances.

Then she ran from behind the bar and avoided the boy she had shot. She passed within inches of me.

I was halfway off the stool, my feet flat on the floor. I thought about many things right then. I thought how here was a young, troubled girl, part of my *raza*, my people, with not much going for her except a pair of damn beautiful eyes. I thought that, except to the poor guy bleeding on the floor, she was more scared and hurt than dangerous. I thought how sometimes you have to give people a break, a second chance. I thought those things.

I tripped her as she ran to the door and she flew head first to the floor. The gun slid from her hand and clunked against a wall.

She looked up and saw the gun I had drawn from the holster under my sweater. Her wonderful eyes begged Maggie, but no help existed behind the bar.

I said, "You're under arrest. You have the right to remain silent. Anything you say . . . "

NEIGHBORHOOD WATCH

The neighborhood has changed over the years, but then hasn't everything? I've changed, that's for sure. When Emilia and I moved in the house we were kids with a kid of our own. That was five children and close to fifty years ago. The house was only a few years old and we paid $5,000 for it. Hard to believe now but that was a bundle back then. It was a struggle but we stayed. Man, oh man, if I had only been able to buy three or four of these houses. For what they go for now? Well, that's water under the bridge or *lo que pasó, voló*, as my father used to say.

We wouldn't have made it except for the job at the brick factory. Working with the Italians eventually turned into a godsend, but when I was hired I was the lowest of the low—the only Mexican guy in the entire place, so I guess they treated me all right, considering.

Funny how life is. The Italians settled into the North Side, built homes and businesses, raised their families, and then the Mexicans started moving in and ten years later most of the Italians were gone and Spanish was spoken everywhere. Emilia and I didn't object, of course, but I will say that those Italian people were solid for the most part. Loyal to a fault. Took care of their homes, kept the yards neat as doctors' offices, and had the best damn church bazaars I ever been to. They had their troublemakers, sure, every group does. That was what was behind the fire bombing of the house on the corner a few months after we moved into our place. Two of the older Italians started a feud with each other and the next thing I know fire trucks are parked all up and down the street. But that was unusual. Like I said, for the most part they were good people who minded their own business.

Sausage sandwiches and beer—you knew it was summer when you could walk over to Mount Carmel and buy a sausage sandwich and a beer for a buck, play some Chuck-A-Luck for a nickel, and all the pretty Italian girls wore red, white or green shorts.

Oh, oh. Starting to sound like an old fart again. Sitting on the porch, on the swing that Emilia and I set up so many years ago, I guess I turn a bit sentimental. Good thing she's not around to see me like this. Spending my days on this swing that doesn't move—frozen stiff from age and rust, just like me—watching the comings and goings of neighbors I don't even know. Some days I don't talk to anyone unless one of the grandkids stops by. They're good kids. They don't speak more than a few words of Spanish, but I always know they're coming to visit when the windows in the house start to vibrate from the music they blast from their cars. Embarrassing, but what can I do? I'm just the old *abuelito*, the little grandfather, living all by myself in this old house, and I should be grateful for the company. Most people think I'm deaf, some think I'm blind, too, and they all think I'm a little *loco* with a touch of that old-timers' disease. Let them think it. *Me vale madre*. What do I care?

And now the neighborhood's changing again.

Guess I wasn't cut out to be a real estate tycoon. I didn't buy me more houses when they were really cheap all those years ago—of course, I couldn't have afforded to buy any more even if I had thought of it—and I never anticipated that my neighborhood, *mi barrio* as we used to call it, would turn into a hot market for young white couples who have at least a hundred grand of credit, want to buy a nice brick home, take care of a yard and live in a part of the city with a real history and a real personality that is close to downtown office jobs. I'm sitting on a gold mine, like my daughter Francine says. But if I sell, then what? She's not going to put me up, we all know that. Anyway, I can still talk to Emilia here, if I set my mind to it, and that's not going to happen anywhere else no matter how nice of an apartment my kids find for me. No, I'm not going anywhere. One day I'll die here on my broken swing and that's the way they'll find me, when they find me. Probably be dead for a couple of days before someone notices that I haven't moved for a spell.

Those two across the street. They're a pair. She's cute. Sara's her name. Likes to wear short shorts and tank tops and work up a sweat in the flowerbeds Carmen Ávila planted around the house back in the seventies. I worry about Carmen and Alfredo and hope they're doing all right up in Northglenn. Hair like a shaft of morning sunshine. Sara across the street, not Carmen. Carmen'd be lucky if she has any hair left.

The husband's a big guy, always dressed in a suit except when he mows the lawn. Drives a flashy sports car. Must be a Miata or something like that, but I thought those cars were for women. What do I know, eh? His name's Carl.

Then there's her boyfriend. Don't know his name. Guy in a silver pickup truck with fancy wheels, fat tires and tinted windows who comes by every other day or so about an hour after the husband leaves for work. Short red-headed young man, but stocky, full of muscles, like he works out. He parks down the street or around the corner, runs into the house, then comes out later, much later, and runs back to his pickup.

Once in a great while the two of them leave together and take off in his ride. Lunch? A drink? Just cruising around? Can't screw every minute I guess.

The couple's lived in the house for only two months, but already they've had four fights that woke me up in the middle of the night, and it takes a lot to wake me up. The sleep of the dead is not easy to disturb. Cops came by a couple of times. And other nights I hear shouting and cursing. That's how I learned their names. That couple is trouble for themselves, for me, for the neighborhood. But what am I going to do about it? *Nada*. Nothing, absolutely nothing.

* * *

Got dark on me. Damn, I must have dozed off and it's night already. Better fix me something to eat. This porch always needed a light. A kid busted the one over the door when we moved in and I never did replace it. At least I thought it was a kid. There was some bad stuff when we moved in, at first, but the Delvecchios, next door, they had a party and invited us and we met almost everyone on the block and that was that. No more bad stuff. No more dirty words painted on the fence, no more ringing doorbells and nobody at the door, no more ugly stares. That party was where I heard about the job at the plant. A move up for me from construction work. Good thing Emilia and I decided to go to that party. Delvecchios were good people.

Oh, oh. The pickup truck is still parked down the street. Very careless, and this late?

And here comes Carl.

Parks his car, doesn't bother to turn off the lights, sprints inside. Now what?

Should take care of that food. I could pass out from not eating, or so said the doctor. Wonder how Sara's dealing with the men in her life.

Um. Sounded like a crash. Something. What the hell? The red-haired guy, sneaking out to his silver pickup.

Where is Carl? And Sara? Nothing. No lights, no sound, *nada*. Guy in the pickup is long gone. Hey. It's their problem, their soap opera.

Damn! That was a window breaking. I heard that. ¡*Santo Niño*! She's screaming. The cops will be here any minute. The whole neighborhood heard that scream.

Need to warm up the beans that Francine brought by, and that little bit of soup left over from yesterday. What's on TV? News. Christ, it is late. How long was I out there?

Ah. Sirens. Here come the cops.

* * *

"Mr. Sánchez, we'd like to ask a few questions, if you don't mind?"

"Sure. What's going on? Somebody in trouble?"

"Well there was some trouble, yes. Tell us, did you see anything out of the usual tonight?"

"Can't say that I did. But then, I'm an old man, and I might miss things that others see, know what I mean?"

"Yeah, sure. Have you seen any strangers around lately, even if you didn't see anything tonight? Maybe some kids hanging around, messing with things they shouldn't?"

"Strangers? Kids? Well, there's always kids around, but I wouldn't call them strangers. Why, what happened?"

"How well you know the Parkers, the people across the street?"

"Don't know them at all. They keep pretty much to themselves, not like the Ávilas who used to live in that house. We were always talking to each other, visiting, sharing stuff. Not these new folks, though. Not like it used to be."

"Yeah, we understand. You didn't know the Parkers and you didn't see anything tonight or anything unusual lately. Sorry we bothered you."

"Uh, Officer. What happened? What was the trouble?"

"Well, if you don't know already you will soon enough. Mr. Parker, Carl Parker, he was killed tonight. His wife said that they had been out to dinner and when they came home they ran into a kid who apparently had broken in to their house. According to Mrs. Parker the kid went crazy. He wanted money, drugs, anything, and when Mr. Parker tried to stop him the kid went after him with a bat that he had taken from Mr. Parker's memorabilia collection. Then the kid took off and Mrs. Parker called us. We're looking for a dark Mexican kid about fifteen wearing a blue baseball cap, jeans and a black T-shirt that had some lettering on it that she thinks said 'Cinco de Mayo' or something like that. Seen anybody matches that description?"

"A Mexican kid? You're joking, right? That's all there are around here. Why would a kid do something like that? Damn, it doesn't make sense."

"That's okay, pop. Nothing these punks do ever makes sense. We'll figure it out. Leave that to us. If you think of anything, or see something in the next day or two, give us a call. Here's my card. Thanks for your help."

He turned, then stopped.

He said, "And maybe you should have your house checked for security. Locks, windows, that kind of thing. We can help. Call us at the station, we got a program, especially for seniors."

Seniors? My ass.

What do you know? A Mexican kid? It's not right. The way these people try to blame others for their mess. Maybe I should have told the cops what I know. They wouldn't believe me. An old man? Old man Sánchez, seeing things. That sweet Sara Parker said it was a Mexican delinquent and that's who the cops are going to find, and when they drag one in front of her, she'll pick him out. Any story I might have told the cops will be dismissed and forgotten. Case closed.

♠♠♠

"Hello, Larry? Larry Delvecchio? Sorry to call so late. This is Joe Sánchez, an old friend of your father's. They called me Mexican Joe."

In those days everyone had a nickname and Mexican Joe was the best they could do for me. I was lucky compared to what they called some of the other guys.

"Sure, Joe. Long time no see. I haven't heard from you in years. Tell the truth, I wasn't sure you were still around. All the old guys are slipping away. But you know that. Say, is anything wrong? Anything I can help out with?"

"Well, as a matter of fact, I do need a favor, Larry."

"Hey, Joe, no problem. My father made it clear just before he passed that I was to take care of the guys, and he told me about all the favors you did for the family, starting with that hot night before I was even born. Just give me the details, Joe, and it's done."

"Thanks, Larry. It means a lot to me, and I appreciate that your father remembered me. I respected him and he respected me, but that's the way it was back then. Listen to me, blubbering like an old man again. Anyway, Larry, it's like this. These people across the street, they been trashing up the neighborhood and now they did something that could ruin it for all of us around here. The woman's husband just died, so he's out of the picture. But her and her boyfriend . . . it would be better for everyone if they left the neighborhood and stayed away, the both of them."

"We'll take care of it, Joe. Give me an address, whatever, then you go to bed. It's late."

***

"Dad, you need to eat better. This meatloaf's still in the fridge. I brought it over last week. I'll have to throw it out now."

"M'*ija*, you worry too much about me. I eat, I sleep, I take walks around the block. I'm all right. Don't worry so much."

"Right, Dad. I'm not sure you can take care of yourself anymore, especially in this neighborhood. It's worse than I remember. There used to be all those Italian gangsters running around when I was little, but now trouble could come from anyone, even the kids. Look at what happened to those poor people across the street."

"I heard about the husband."

"Not just him, Dad. The wife, too."

"What? Something else?"

"It was in the paper, Dad, if you'd read something besides the comics once in a while. She disappeared. Gone. Her sister from Chicago's been trying to get a hold of her and finally she called the police. They can't find her. No trace. She left everything in the house and just took off. They think she might have gone up into the mountains and killed herself. Grief-stricken over her husband. Something like that."

"*¡Qué carambada!* I didn't know. I hadn't seen her for a few days, but I had no idea. Maybe you're right about this neighborhood."

"Absolutely." She stood against the counter, looking at the few dirty dishes in the sink. "Dad, these windows are filthy." A pause. "Oh-oh. Check this out. Some people think the streets are a junk yard. That pickup's still parked down the block. It's been there for days and nobody's moved it. I'm calling somebody down at City Hall. Have the damn thing towed if I have to."

"Good idea, *m'ija.* Don't want any trash in the neighborhood. Starts with an abandoned car and then who knows where it could lead."

MURDER MOVIE

Marie handed me the jacket, pants and hat and tried not to laugh as she did it.

"When I volunteered to help with the festival," I said, "I didn't think it would mean driving people around. I'm not a chauffeur."

"Quit complaining, Miguel," she answered with a big smile. "This is a great opportunity for you. You're the one that wants to be in the movie business, no? The Latino Film Festival puts you right in the middle of the action with people who can help you. Don't be stupid. Impress people with your commitment to the festival, to helping out. Mingle, talk to them so they know who you are. It could lead somewhere. What else you got going that you can't spare one weekend to take care of some producers, directors and actors, and see free movies, too? Seize the day, pal."

What Marie said made sense, of course, but I didn't want to listen. She may have been a friend, even a girlfriend once upon a time, and she may have managed to get a sweet job at Channel 7 in the news department, and she still may have looked real good all dressed up for work, but I thought she had done me wrong with this festival thing. When she told me she could get me on the volunteer list for the festival, I had jumped at the chance. I thought I could moderate some of the directors' panels, or introduce a couple of the films, talk to Eddie Olmos or Andy García about my screenplay and maybe entertain one of the cute Latina starlets in between screenings.

That's what I expected, that's not what happened.

The day before anything official started, I had to pick up a few Hollywood wannabes at the airport, at some very strange hours I thought, then get them to the hotel and squeeze in a few trips to dinner for groups of AIPs (almost important people). Then, on Friday, I waited for them at their hotel until they were good and ready, trucked them to the theater, waited around to drive them to the receptions, and then later back to the hotel. I was stuck up front in the limo, and my only interaction with my passengers was an occasional hello or thank you or hey, slow down, we don't want to die in Denver. I deserved more respect than that, even if I was only twenty-five, but there was no one to gripe to except Marie, and she quickly tired of my "whiny act."

I managed. That was my attitude. I could survive anywhere, do anything, if I had to. I kept a grin on my face although the silly uniform I had to wear was too damn bulky for the Colorado springtime sunshine. I said yes sir and no ma'am, got headaches from the perfume and liquor breaths and did not get any sleep that first night before I had to be back at it early Saturday morning and do it all over again.

By Saturday night, I was exhausted and cranky. The day had been hot, the passengers had not been in good moods since they were all nervous about the audience reaction to their movies and I had not made any meaningful connections with anybody. The job had been a bust and then it got worse when Marie called me on the car phone and begged me to do one more drive that night, after the last film. I argued, but in the end I gave in because she promised to make it up to me and the way she said "make it up to you" was enough to re-energize my tired bones and dormant libido.

I agreed to drive a producer and his actress wife to a late dinner meeting with a group of local Hispanics (among my friends, Hispanics means Mexicans with money) who wanted to play Hollywood. The concept was enough to make me gag, but I kept my smile as I waited in front of the hotel for my passengers.

She twirled through the revolving doors and I immediately knew it was Mrs. Castillo. Short red dress, bright red lipstick, a black top that had to be some kind of lingerie not quite covering her ample bosom and the sweetest accent I had heard since my cousin Cristina from Matamoros had stayed with us one summer and learned a few English words.

Debra Castillo used to be Dee Luna, the sexpot who had a decent career in Mexican B movies. The plots of her flicks usually involved singing stock-car racers or rodeo cowboys. She had an affair with a Chicano senator from California, and that led to an appearance in a Robert Rodríguez project. Her life changed with that small part. There's one classic scene that produced a memorable poster and about a million downloads on the Internet. She stands in the desert, the wind lifting her skirt in all directions, and she blows a kiss to the Yankee pilot as he takes off in his biplane to hunt down Pancho Villa. Her gringo lover loses control of the plane after Pancho has riddled it with Gatling gunfire, and the desperation in her eyes as she watches the plane spin in fiery descent was enough to get her more and better parts. In just a few years she had graced the cover of every magazine that catered to movie fans, Latinos or men who like to ogle attractive women. She was the current Mrs. Reynaldo Castillo. Her husband was one of the few Cuban-American producers in Hollywood and one of the few producers of any heritage who could bankroll a movie all by himself, if he had to.

I opened the passenger door for her, and she gave me a breathless, "*Gracias, jovencito*." Her entrance into the car was anything but glamorous, and I had to help her with a polite push. I did get an eyeful of a pair of tanned thighs that would have made me stay for a double feature, but she didn't seem to notice or care.

A few minutes later the husband stormed through the same revolving doors. He practically ran to the car and jumped in. I was closing the door when he grabbed it and jerked it shut. By the time I had made it to the driver's seat, they were in a full-fledged shouting match that even the massive body of the Lincoln could not contain. I spied on them in the rearview mirror, but they were so intent on drowning out each other that they did not stop even when I pulled away from the curb. I did not need to talk to them anyway. I had my directions and I knew the address.

They were meeting the investor group at an expensive restaurant in the foothills about thirty miles away, and I had an hour to get them there. I bitched about the drive to Marie, but she explained that the money people from Boulder didn't want to drive into Denver. And one of them owned the restaurant. An out-of-the-way place for a serious discussion about Latino movie-making in the brand new century—that's what Marie told me when she filled me in on the details of my task.

I drove through the city streets to the interstate, cut to the Boulder Turnpike for several minutes, and then off the highway onto a gravel road into the hills and the secluded nature reserve that surrounded the restaurant.

I thought I saw him slap her and I did see her break into tears at least twice. They finally stopped arguing about a mile from the restaurant when she tried to rearrange her makeup, without much luck.

I stopped the limo and opened the door for them, but only he got out. He turned in her general direction and said, "Quit the games, Dee. I'm not doing this anymore. Either you come in now or you can find another way back to the hotel. Hell, you can find another way back to L.A."

I heard her answer: "*¡Cabrón! ¡Déjame!*"

Mr. Castillo must have understood that to mean that he would have to go to the meeting by himself and he chugged off, mumbling under his breath.

I still held the door, so I leaned in and said, "You okay? Anything I can do?"

"*¿Habla español?*" she asked in return.

"Uh, *lo siento*," I stammered. "*Por favor*. I'm Chicano, *pero*, uh, I don't speak Spanish very well."

"That's all right. I can manage in English. At least I think I can." She coughed, and I thought she was going to cry again.

"You sure you're all right? Did he hurt you?"

"No. No. Not really. Not this time."

I felt very strange feeling sorry for one of the most beautiful women in the world, whose make-up was smeared and whose dress kept inching up her legs and whose angry husband was less than fifty yards away in a high-powered meeting that could have determined my future. I wanted to be in that meeting. I wanted to pitch my script. It was the right audience: influential and wealthy Latinos who should want to hear from a young Chicano writer who had a story about murder and lust and revenge among the Hispanic middle class. It was a natural. A murder movie with a Latino slant. But I hadn't been invited to that meeting so I had to be satisfied with soothing the very upset Mrs. Castillo.

Not that it was tough duty. Smeared make-up or not, she was easy on the eyes, as Bogart might have said in "The Big Sleep," and I thought that I should at least try to calm her down.

"Has he hurt you before?"

She didn't answer right away. She didn't want to answer, I could see that, and that told me all I needed to know. The mighty Reynaldo Castillo beat up his wife.

"It's not that important. The fights aren't what I'm afraid of. That's not it. I wish that was all."

I shut the door, walked around the car and sat behind the steering wheel. I slid open the glass that separated the passengers from the driver and watched her for a few minutes. She seemed better, more in control.

I said, "If you don't mind me asking, what is it? What are you afraid of?"

She hesitated again. It was difficult for her to speak but it wasn't the language problem that was getting in her way. Why should she trust me with the secrets of her heart, with the pain of a marriage that obviously hadn't worked out? I was just the limo man, the driver, not even a real chauffeur, and she knew it and she had every reason to tell me to mind my own business.

She finally said, "One of Rey's wives was murdered by a man who broke into their home. They never found the killer. Rey's first wife disappeared after the divorce. She's been missing for years. I think Rey had them both killed. It's crazy, I know. But he's a macho like from the old days, and he's rich. Can't bear to think that any woman would stand up to him, much less leave him. He thinks every woman wants his money. He's mean, cruel. *¡Un bruto!* If I told you what he does, you wouldn't believe it. No one believes it. He's famous, generous, a leader of the community. I'm the Mexican bimbo—I know that's what they call me. No one listens to me. No one believes me."

I wanted to reach over and hug her, tell her that I, for one, believed her, and that I would take her away right then and there to wherever she wanted to go. But, as I thought about what I would say, it sounded so lame even to me that I could not dredge up the courage to say it to her. She started crying again, and I listened and watched in helplessness. I shut the partition and gave her some privacy.

The meeting took a little bit more than an hour, and he scarcely acknowledged her as he climbed in the car. I guess he forgot about making her catch another ride. He made several short calls with his cell phone, then leaned back as though he wanted to sleep.

The drive started out quietly enough. I concentrated on the dark road because it had no street lights, homes or other evidence of human activity. We were on the edge of a slight rise in the hill that gave the appearance of a steep drop to the meadow below. The isolated stretch continued for only a few miles but it took my complete attention to keep the bulky limo on the narrow dirt strip. The return trip seemed longer than on the way in. My eyes aren't the best, especially at night, and in the hills, with only dust covered headlights and dim moonlight to guide me, I was practically aiming the car by instinct and memory only. And I was dog tired.

The gunshot echoed in the tight confines of the limo. I jerked and twisted the steering wheel, slammed the brakes. The car swerved and died. I thought someone from outside had shot at the car but when I turned to my passengers, I saw Castillo doubled over in pain, holding his shoulder. Blood seeped through his suit jacket. She cringed in the corner of the seat, crying, whispering incoherently.

"What the . . . !"

I jumped out. Dust floated around the car from my abrupt stop. I ran to the passenger side, opened Castillo's door and stared at his wound. It looked bad but what did I know? Her slim fingers held a gun, gingerly, almost as though she were not touching it. I reached over her groaning husband and took the gun from her.

"He tried to kill me." She was almost too calm. "He was going to shoot me in this car, and you, too. I was trying to holler for you to stop, but he covered my mouth with his hand. I grabbed at anything I could and I must have somehow turned the gun. And then, I don't know how, the gun went off, and he shot himself." She sobbed, then repeated, "He tried to kill me."

I aimed the gun at him. He stopped squirming in the back seat long enough to see that I was now in charge.

He shouted at me, although I was only a few inches from his face.

"*¡Imbécil!* Don't listen to her! She shot me. I'm the one bleeding! She had the gun, not me. You took the gun from her! Call the police. Use my phone." Air squeezed through his thin, white lips.

I thought he was passing out.

"She told me all about you," I said. "I will call the cops. Get out where I can keep an eye on you."

It took an eternity but he finally crawled out of the car. He was in obvious pain, and the blood would not stop even though his knuckles were locked on his shoulder.

"You've got to help me. I could bleed to death. There must be a first aid kit in this car. Get something that will stop the bleeding."

I waited for her to respond. She shook her head.

"Don't do anything he says. He's going to kill us. Let him rot here. Let's go. Let's get away while we can."

Castillo laughed and I thought that was the most unreal part of a very unreal night.

He said, "Dee, you're good. A better actress than anyone gives you credit for. What's your plan, baby? Get this kid to finish me off, then you take care of him and claim that he tried to rob us? Is that it? Not bad. But, it'll never work. You've got to get the gun back from this guy, and I don't think that's going to happen. Right, kid?"

We stood along the edge of the headlight beams and I was having a hard time making out any details. He was moving so slowly that I knew it would take several minutes for him to reach the direct glare of the headlights. I had to watch the both of them at once. I held the gun on him but I tried to keep her in my vision, too. It was all a jumble, a mass of confusion in my head. I had to think clearly.

He was right about one thing. She was an actress, and I had to remember that.

"Kid, I need help," Castillo said. "I'm going to faint. You must do something. *¡Ayúdame, hombre!* She's a witch. Watch her. Don't turn your back on her. See what she did to me."

She moved closer, and I jerked the gun in her direction and waved her away from me. Then I quickly re-aimed the gun at the wounded man. I could not see their faces and I realized that I was incredibly hot and that sweat dripped across my eyes. I should have taken off the chauffeur's jacket but it was too late for that.

"Don't listen to him," she almost whispered. "Let's just leave him and go. You can call the police after we drive away. He's up to something."

I wiped my face with my free hand and I began to put it together. What she said did it for me. Her words clicked and my brain made all the necessary connections at once. Why wait to call the cops? Did she want to do something before the cops showed up? Maybe shoot me while my attention was diverted, then finish off her husband? He was the one bleeding, right? How had she managed to get the gun away from him in the first place? And why would he have a gun when he was going to a business meeting? She had to have had the gun all the time, in that fancy purse she had carried all night. She had played me, that was obvious. She was a beautiful woman, toying with a kid who had been dazzled by her cleavage and legs. I had almost fallen for it.

I pointed the gun at her.

I said, "Okay, enough. No one's going anywhere. I'll call the cops and we'll wait for them to come and sort this out. You just stay there, please."

I motioned with the gun for her to stand still.

She bit her lower lip. "Don't do this," she said. "You don't know him."

I shook my head because now I understood completely.

I said to Castillo, "Hand me your phone."

"Certainly," he said from between clenched teeth. "Take it."

He moved slowly, pulling the phone from his suit coat pocket. I reached for the phone with my left hand and when I touched its plastic case, I relaxed the hold on the gun in my right hand. I realized my fingers ached from holding the gun in a vise grip and I did not want to have any accidents. I was close to him, closer than I wanted to be, but I had to get the phone. I paid more attention to dealing with the phone than to the man or the woman, or to the direction the gun was pointed. That's when he grabbed my jacket lapels with his blood-smeared left hand, jerked me forward and kneed me in the stomach. I felt dizzy, sick. I fell backwards and dropped the gun.

He picked it up and aimed it at me. I heard her scream. I lay on my back in the dirt, unable to catch my breath, the sweat on my skin suddenly ice cold. My lips quivered and almost everything disappeared—the woman in the red dress, the man bleeding all over his thousand-dollar suit, the limo, the night. All I could see was the barrel of the gun, and it made me smile. The gun roared and I twitched but I still smiled. I should have seen it coming. I had the same ending in my screenplay.

BAD HAIRCUT DAY

César shook my snipped hair from his striped barber cloth. "How long I been clippin' you, Michael?"

"Ah, geez," I answered as I grabbed my coat from the hook on the wall. "At least fifteen years. I just happened to come in. I was on my way to an interview for my first lawyer job. You were still over at the Bryant Building. I needed a last minute touch-up and you fit me in."

"Yeah, I remember you that day," he said. "That interview had you uptight like a virgin groom. Time flies, don't it?"

I experienced my first César haircut when I was in my late twenties. The air was cool and crisp, an early fall in the city, and I thought I looked respectable in my one and only blue suit and thin gray overcoat. I pushed against the glass revolving door of the building where I wanted to work and caught the reflection of my slightly overgrown hair on top of my ears. Too ragged for a first-year associate in one of Denver's largest law firms, especially for a first impression of a second-generation Mexican American trying to break into big time lawyering. I was early for the interview, of course, so I turned around and dashed into the only barber shop I saw. César Sánchez obliged me with a quick, clean and tidy haircut.

I landed that job and César landed a steady customer, although back then I sometimes went several weeks between cuts.

César brushed off the chair. He said, "You take care and I'll see you next time."

"You bet, César."

I handed him a twenty and waved away his offer to return the five dollars of change. It was a ritual we went through at the end of each of my haircuts.

I left his shop thinking about how the relationship between César and me had changed over the years. For the most part it had been a natural, evolutionary process.

I advanced through the ranks of the practice of commercial law and climbed the ladder of achievement, one moneyed rung at a time. It took time, as anything worthwhile must, but I kept at it. My haircuts became more regular—every twelve days, an automatic appointment—and periodically I treated myself to one of César's haircut and shave specials.

Meanwhile, César's Hair Palace grew from a one chair, one barber stand to a busy, noisy establishment with a shoe shine guy who claimed to be a veteran of some sort. César eventually moved the business and added two chairs, including one for Angel, a brassy, humorous woman. After years of six-day weeks, no vacations, personally opening and closing the shop, and doing everything from sweeping the hair clippings to updating the magazines, César earned the right to serve only his preferred list of customers. My seniority as a client put me on that valuable list.

The Palace sat on Seventeenth Street in the midst of Denver's high-rises. His customers tended to be lawyers, bankers and other men who wore suits every day. The judges and financial consultants treated César like a friend, and when I finally had a little bit of standing in that community of old boys I talked him up. I soon realized he was so well-known downtown that he didn't need any promotion from me.

His haircuts were always right, perfect even. Bottom line, he did what the customer wanted, not what he thought the client needed. He'd make recommendations, sure, but if someone really wanted a fade or a crewcut or maybe a Jordan, that's what César gave him. He was meticulous about completely brushing off a customer's shirt, didn't mind adding a bit of gel or spray, if necessary, and he encouraged customers to make last minute suggestions. And, yet, each haircut took nineteen minutes, sometimes less. It was amazing but he was that capable.

He wasn't much older than I, but I could see that life had been a different kind of struggle for him. A large chunk of that struggle was out in the open. His forearms sported amateur-looking tattoos, and a bent nose sat in the middle of his oblong face.

His clothes invariably were sharp and well-tailored, and his own hair style never varied—swept back, every strand in place, a nice sheen. His gray streaks came long before my hair started to turn, and he joked with me about that. He'd say, "That's a healthy head of hair, Michael. Be grateful and take care of it. Or I might have to cut it all off."

César could tell great stories about all the personalities who had come through his place over the years—sports stars, actors, politicians. But I had a tough time learning anything about him. He was close-mouthed when it came to his own story. He had been raised on the Western Slope, labored in the onion and sugar beet fields as a child, spent some time "out East," was married and had a couple of sons. If I asked about his family, he answered quickly and decisively, "They're doin' good." And that would be all. He would go into one of his stories and the small talk about him would be abandoned.

He kept the mood light with jokes and Broncos updates but when he had to be, he was all business, once in a while a bit impatient, especially with salesmen who wouldn't accept no. His leathery skin would flush. His clenched fists would hang rigidly at his sides. His lips would curl around his teeth. And the salesman would rush out.

I knew to be on time for my appointments. I had this love-fear dynamic going on with my barber, and it didn't seem strange to me.

I changed firms a couple of times, bought a few more suits, and it would have been more convenient for me to use the trendy hair salon on the first floor of the office building where I finally settled. But I stayed with César. He hadn't raised his prices to extravagant levels, and I knew what I was going to get from him. No surprises. I simply sat in the chair and he would do his magic without any instructions from me. We understood each other.

I unfailingly left his shop feeling good about myself, good about my life. How many barbers can do that? A good barber is hard to find.

César hit me up for legal help only once. Everyone from my mechanic to my kid's second-grade teacher eventually asked for my "opinion" or a "little bit of advice" or, anxiously, out-and-out representation. César the barber did it the one time, and that was after I had been his customer for ten years, and it wasn't for him. César's friend, Abel, had been busted on a narcotics rap. César was concerned that Abel not be talked into anything that he would later regret. He was worried that Abel might be pressured to plead out to something that the district attorney couldn't prove, or agree to a plea bargain that meant he had to testify against his cohorts.

We discussed his friend one evening after César had closed for the day. I had been his last appointment and César said he wanted to talk about something important. He produced a couple of beers from his back room, and I made myself comfortable in one of his barber chairs.

He explained his friend's circumstances, then he made his pitch.

"I know you don't do criminal law, Michael. But I was hopin' that you could steer Abel to an attorney that will treat him right. I grew up with Abel, we picked peaches together when we were kids, over in Palisades. I'd hate to see him railroaded. He ain't a snitch, but when it looks like you don't have a choice, some men will do stupid things."

I didn't hesitate with my response.

"Chris Morales is a good friend. He's top gun, one of the best defense attorneys in the state, hell, in the country. If he takes a case he pulls out all the stops. Whatever he does for your friend, you can believe it will be the best he can get, from anyone."

He nodded.

"That's what I'm talkin' about," he said. "I'm not sayin' Abel's a saint, but he's also a family man, never hurt no one. This drug business is out of character for him. And it's his first serious arrest, so there must be somethin' that can be worked out. I'm just afraid the prosecutor will take advantage of him. Abel ain't exactly the brightest candle on the cake."

"Chris is expensive," I said. "You get what you pay for, César. Can your friend take care of that?"

"That's on me, Michael. Like I said, I grew up with this guy. We're practically related. I think of him like a brother. He's done favors for me in the past, it's almost like I owe him. So, you tell your friend that he sends his bill to me. I'm good for it."

"It's going to be steep. I hope you can swing it."

He shook my hand as though we were closing a deal.

"You let me worry about that," he said. "I won't embarrass you with your lawyer chum. I pay my debts. Just one thing, Michael."

"What would that be?"

"I'm countin' on you to keep an eye on your man, Chris. I know he'll do a great job and that Abel will land on his feet. But if you could just stay on top of it, I would appreciate that. Okay?"

I agreed and I did what César asked. I was glad I could help César.

Chris took the case, primarily because he thought Abel had illegal search issues that needed to be aired out in the courtroom. César covered all the bills, including expensive pre-trial experts and forensic tests on the seized drugs. Chris filed motion after motion and scheduled numerous hearings. The prosecution ran out of steam after about nine months of intense legal scrimmages. Abel pleaded to a minor possession charge and walked away. No major conviction, no jail time, no need to turn against his pals, who remained unknown to everyone except Abel.

César overwhelmed me with gratitude for the favorable resolution of his friend's legal problems. The free haircut was more than I expected. I felt that I had raised my standing in his eyes although I hadn't done anything except give him a referral, something I did every week for others who never thought twice about it.

We chugged along in our respective roles: César the barber, the downtown icon, who needed visibility to stay in the game, to compete; and Michael, the high-powered corporate lawyer who valued his privacy and whose clients preferred that their lawyer stay out of the spotlight.

A few years after Abel's case, I showed up unexpectedly at the Palace. It was another fine Colorado autumn morning, just like the first time I met César. I had an arbitration in Dallas later in the week, which meant that I would have to miss my regular appointment. I thought that I would stop by and reschedule or, with some luck, finagle a quick trim if César could fit me in.

It was early, not quite nine, his normal opening time. The door was unlocked but the shop looked empty. I figured César was checking his books in the back office, the one with a sign on the door that warned, "Employees Only!"

I strolled in, picked out the current issue of *Time* from his rack, sat down and waited. Several minutes passed and the situation started to bug me. I thought I heard muffled breathing on the other side of the door to the office.

I half-heartedly hollered, "César, you open?" Nothing.

I reluctantly gave up on the magazine and César, and started to leave.

The office door burst open. I fell back in my chair. César tumbled through the doorway screaming, "Run!" Before I could react, César tripped and sprawled to the floor. A guy wearing a ski mask pointed a gun at César, then at me.

I shouted, "What the . . . ?"

The guy in the mask shouted back, "Shut up! On the floor!"

I looked at César and he nodded and indicated with his eyes that I should do what the gunman ordered.

I slipped off the chair and laid down on César's cool tile floor.

César said, "Let this guy go. He's not part of this. It makes it worse for you." He was calm, contained.

The words didn't register with me. They weren't what I expected.

The gunman stood over us, still working that gun for all it was worth.

"Yeah, sure," he said. "You bet I'll let this guy walk out of here. This is your fault, C. This is your mess. All you had to do was treat me right. But, old habits, right C? I knew you'd rip me off."

I couldn't put it together but the guy's implied threat cut any bravado I might have had stored deep in my gut. My nerve drained away and I started to sweat. I heard César and the gunman talking but they didn't make any sense. The pounding in my ears didn't make any sense either.

The gunman put his gun against my temple. His eyes peered through the slits in the ski mask—red-veined, dilated pupils that moved constantly. I felt the hard barrel push the side of my head. My breath came shallow and fast.

César kicked the back of the man's knees. The gunman grunted and fell in a heap.

The gun clattered next to me. César leaped to his feet and jumped on the man, punching and kicking him furiously. As the blows rained on the gunman, a stream of ugly epithets flowed from César's mouth, in Spanish and English.

He shouted, "*¡Cabrón, puto!* You try to take me?! You try to pull this two-bit bullshit?!"

He didn't stop the beating until the man went limp and passed out. It had lasted less than a minute. The mask had ripped away from the gunman's head. Blood flowed from his eyes, nose and mouth.

César took three deep breaths. He picked up the gun. He looked at me, shook his head. He hung the "Closed" sign on the door, turned the lock and shut the blinds. He said, "Help me with this." He lifted the man's shoulders, I grabbed the legs and we half-carried, half-dragged the unconscious gunman to the back room. I tried not to look at the blood.

César said, "Any minute now the rest of my crew will start showin' up. Don't make any noise. Even if you hear them at the door. Except for Angel, they don't have keys. Fred and Oscar always expect me or Angel to let them in. Watch that this *pendejo* don't come to." He pointed at an aluminum baseball bat lying on the floor. "Use that if you have to. If he starts movin' hit him hard, right on top of the head."

I picked up the bat. It felt heavy and awkward in my hand but I gripped it solidly and was ready to do what César wanted.

With his left hand César flipped open a cell phone and punched in numbers. His right hand held the gun.

After a few seconds he said, "Angel? . . . Yeah. Rudy showed up. . . . I took care of it. You on your way? . . . Yeah. . . . Okay, okay. . . . No, nothin'. . . . Yeah. . . . Look, I know. What can I do? I told you he was up to somethin' stupid. He had to be. . . . No, I'll finish it. Call Fred and Oscar. Now. Tell them we're closed today—there's a gas leak or somethin' like that. I'll get back to you."

Then it was his turn to listen to her. Several times he started and stopped what he wanted to say. When he finally could say it completely, it came out as, "I said I will take care of it. That means I will take care of it. All of it." His eyes focused on me. "You handle Fred and Oscar."

He closed his phone, jammed it in his shirt pocket.

The blood in my brain finally started to flow again. I said, "What the hell is going on? Who is this guy? What are you into?"

César shrugged his shoulders. He stared at me. He shrugged again. The man on the floor groaned, turned on his side. César kicked him in the jaw. The man quivered, then was still. Blood and drool dripped from his lips. I dropped the bat.

"Take it easy," I said. "You're gonna kill this guy. What was it? A holdup, a burglary? You catch him in the act? Whatever, it isn't worth killing him." Then I had a brilliant flash of wisdom. "We should call the cops."

César made a sound that I guess was supposed to be a laugh. It came out too horrible for that, though.

"You been a good customer, Michael. You're solid—I can see that. The way you handled Abel's trouble showed me that. You're not like some of the geeks who parade through here. For a lawyer your head's screwed on tight, your heart's in the right place, most of the time. Your roots are strong, same as mine. You never ask too many questions, you show respect, you don't talk down." He paused, examined the gun. "For all that, you deserve a break. You walk out of here and forget anythin' you saw and the next time you come in for your regular, we don't bring this up. Like it never happened. You hear me, Michael? Nothin' happened. You shouldn't even be here anyways. So, maybe you were never here today? I think that's the way we do this." He paused again. "I'll take care of this guy."

My tongue ran over the words I wanted to say but I pushed them out.

"I can't believe it, you talking like that. I have to go to the police. You know that. I saw the whole thing going down. He was trying to hold you up. He had the gun, he threatened you, me. He would have shot us if you hadn't jumped him. You have nothing to worry about, César. No D.A. will file charges, no jury would convict you of anything. Colorado has the Make-My-Day law—what you did fits right in with that. I'm your witness, I'm . . . "

He waved the gun in my face and I shut up.

"Michael, you don't understand. I'm givin' you an option. Take it, while you can. You don't have to be involved. Maybe you shouldn't, right? You're a partner in the firm now. Right? You need this kind of publicity? You want to be interviewed by the cops, the D.A.? Have to do depositions, subpoenas, maybe lie detector tests if the defense attorney really gets into it. Testify at a trial? I don't think you need all that. "

It was gibberish. He was trying to eliminate me from the scene and he was saying anything that popped in his head that he thought might sway me. He was saying everything except the truth.

I asked, "Why you doing this? What's your connection to this guy?"

César snapped open the gun, looked through the chamber, shut it, then stuck it in the waistband of his pants.

He said, "I know Rudy for a long time. We used to be . . . uh . . . roommates. We have a partnership, an ongoin' arrangement from years ago. He thought I didn't treat him right—maybe not accountin' for all the profits, from his point of view. Guys like him are like that. Don't trust nobody because they can't be trusted, and they know it. He showed up today in that dumbass mask and wanted to collect what he thought was his, and what I know he ain't earned. You saw how it played out. Now, I have to clean it up. Like I said, you don't want to be involved with this. You walk out now, never mention it to no one and it's like it ain't never happened. For what it's worth, you can take my word on that. I got no beef with you. Angel will do what I say. You really are an innocent bystander. But you have to cooperate."

He let all that sink in.

The barber opened a narrow door in the corner of the office. He pulled out a mop, bucket and a box of trash bags.

"I'm asking for some leeway from you," he said as he shut the broom closet door. He picked up a pair of scissors, shook his head and put them back on his desk. "Maybe 'cause you been comin' in here for so long." He stared at me and I had to look away. "Maybe 'cause we know each other on the side of my life that shouldn't mix with this side of my life."

I looked back at him. He pointed his chin at Rudy's bloody face.

We were interrupted by a knock on the front door. I started to say something, stopped myself, walked away from César and the unconscious man. Behind me César grunted as he moved Rudy's body. I heard the thunk of Rudy's head bumping the bucket.

Dan Riley, a young assistant district attorney who wanted a position in my firm, waited at the outer door. I quickly opened it, eased out and shut it behind me.

Riley looked surprised. "Hey, Michael," he said. "How are you? Is César open or . . . ?"

He glanced at the closed sign hanging on the door then came back to me with the unfinished question in his eyes.

I said, "Uh, he has to . . . to take off, probably won't be back today. Some kind of emergency, a gas leak or something, somewhere. Not sure. I was just trying to change my appointment. You might want to call him tomorrow, see what's up."

Riley nodded, muttered, "Damn." He said the things that he thought were necessary to keep his name on the list of potential future associates in my firm. I participated in the charade, did my part, until finally he went on with his business. I ran back to my office.

I had to spend a few hours on the phone and I ended up indebted to a jerk Texas lawyer but I managed to postpone the Dallas arbitration. I needed to keep my regular appointment with César. I did not want him to think that I had moved on to another barber. A good barber is hard to find.

BACKUP

It's not that I thought Dad was a creep just because he was a cop. It was weird, that's all. He'd be out busting the bad guys, getting worked up behind the stuff he had to see every day like women all bruised and black-eyed, and burned kids and old men pistol-whipped. And the dead people. He saw plenty of those. He did that for years, and he started drinking heavy, a regular booze hound. And I remember him coming home in his uniform and before he hit the bottle he'd take off his gun, unload and wipe it clean, and tell me and my brother Martín that if he ever caught us fooling around with his piece that he would "kick the living hell out of us." We were like seven and ten so that scared us, of course, and made us want to get our hands on that gun all that much more. We never did, though. He kept it locked up and the key stayed with him. When he eventually took us target shooting and tried to teach us how to deal with a gun, he jammed us with rules. "Never load a gun unless you intend to use it. Never point a gun at anyone unless you intend to hurt them. Never shoot at someone unless you intend to kill that person." His favorite rule? "Stop. Look. Be careful. Be aware of where you are and who's around." By the time he preached his rules, we had moved on and it was no big deal. And by the time I made it to Cunningham High, no one hardly ever brought up Dad's cop job.

That was before Dad made detective and before Martín was arrested and sent to the Youth Correctional Facility, or the YCF, as the old man called it. I missed that guy, but truth is, he was a mess-up, big time. Martín never grew up, never figured out what to do with himself, and when he got into drugs, that was it for my big brother. Now, he's sitting out his sentence. The judge showed no mercy (even though Dad was on the force) and sentenced him to farm work and boredom at the YCF until he turned eighteen. That was the first time I knew that my mother's heart was broken. *Pinche* judge, like my Dad said, just loud enough for the asshole to hear him. But Martín will get out later this year. Whether he wants to come home is another question. What's there to come home to, right?

The second time my mom broke down was when they pressured Dad off the force. Even I did not see that coming. And then they started fighting all the time until he moved out and they filed for divorce. And there I was, trying to finish high school when I didn't really care about nothing, Dad turned into a stranger, my mom wouldn't quit crying and life was like one big drag.

But I didn't mean for this to be a downer. I like to write in my journal and so I just let it rip; whatever pops in my head ends up in my book. Sometimes it comes out all cheery and sappy and sometimes I can't believe the stuff I put down. I been doing it for years but not even Jamey knows about it. He'd just say that it's so gay, but I know it's what I need to chill sometimes, and gay ain't got nothing to do with it.

Jamey's real name is Jaime Rodríguez, but no one calls him that. And I'm Miguel Reséndez, but you can call me Mike. Mike and Jamey—we been buds since he moved to El-town (our neighborhood is Elvin Heights, but it's been known as El-town from the years when the OGs cruised Braxton Avenue in their low-rider Chevys and Mercurys). He sauntered into Mrs.

Hyde's second-grade class looking like a tall, skinny version of George Lopez, all dark and big-headed. Jamey and Mike—Cheech and Chong. That's what some of the jocks call us, behind our backs, but we don't care.

Jamey and I are a good team. He's tough, not afraid to mix it up if he has to. We've had to back each other up a few times, usually against the El-town Cutters. They finally left us alone, but there were plenty of times when Jamey and I had to throw down. We been knocked out, cut up, even shot at, but we never gave in. So now there's a truce between us and the Cutters, and most of the guys who used to hassle us are getting beat up by my brother in the YCF, or cruisin' in their wheelchairs, or dead. It's all good now. Except that my life still sucks.

Jamey and I talked one day a few weeks after Dad split.

"You don't know where he is?" Jamey said, although I think he knew the answer.

"Him and Mom had a big fight. He ran out of the house saying that everyone could shove it. He must have gotten drunk. He came home the next morning, early. I could hear him stumbling around. But he didn't stay long. He moved out. It's like he blames us because he screwed up. What I really don't like is that he won't talk to us, he won't explain what's going on with him."

Jamey shrugged. We had skipped last period and were sitting around our table in Corey Park, the place where we wasted a lot of time, sometimes with others from school but most often just the two of us.

"What do you think happened? Didn't your pops say nothing?" Jamey spoke like he was picking his words all careful. I didn't answer right away. I looked at the carved heart with the initials AB/MR that I had carved into the table months ago, when me and Andrea were still an item. "You got to admit, that was extreme, even for your old man." I jerked my head and glared at Jamey. Where was he going with this? "I mean, shooting Cold Play when he didn't have any gun. He's a clown and all that, but still."

I pushed Jamey off the table bench.

"Shut up!" I never had been mad at Jamey, but I was pissed right then, real pissed. Me and Dad weren't exactly Father and Son of the Year, but he was my old man, and no one had a right to talk about him except me.

"Hey, dude. Damn. Cool it." Jamey picked himself up. He clenched his fists, then let it go. "Catch you later, jerk face." He walked away. I almost shouted at him to come back. Almost.

* * *

The night it all came down, I was alone in the house. Mom's text said that she was visiting Grandma Herrera over in Clifton; she might stay the night, something about Grandma not feeling well. Dad apparently had stopped by, there was a dirty plate and half-filled coffee pot on the counter, but he hadn't stayed or left a message.

I felt sick, like the flu or something. I listened to a mix of Dad's oldies. *Too many tear drops for one heart to be crying. You're gonna cry ninety-six tears. Cry, cry, cry.* I had always liked that song even though it made no sense. What was so bad about ninety-six tears? I turned off the CD player and sat in the dark and the silence. I thought about throwing up, or maybe smoking a cigarette, but I didn't do anything. I just sat there, for a long time.

Finally, I switched on a lamp and picked up a newspaper from the end table where it had gathered dust for weeks. *MAN SHOT BY POLICE EXPECTED TO RECOVER.* A smaller headline announced: *Reséndez on Administrative Leave*. I didn't have to read the story to know what else it said.

Officer Reséndez and his partner, Sandra Moreno, were driving through the alleys in the Horseback Hill area when they saw a man crawl out of a basement window and sneak through a back yard. The police officers waited in the darkness and made their arrest.

Slam-dunk. Dad and his partner Sandra must have been all smiles. They had busted Hank García, the so-called Zebra Burglar because he wore a black-and-white bandanna around his head. The cops wanted that guy, for months. The story was that he and his gang had broken into hundreds of homes and businesses over the past two years, and some people had been hurt, seriously.

But the arrest went bad. They were calling in the details when Fred Jackson showed up. He was a low-life most of us knew as a cheap hood who gave himself the nickname "Cold Play." According to García, Dad immediately left the car and started waving his gun at Cold Play. *I was sitting in the back seat, handcuffed. The cop and this other guy were saying something behind the car, I don't know what. It sounded like an argument. Then I heard the blast of a gun and it seemed like the whole inside of the car lit up. I twisted around to my left and I could see the cop holding his gun, standing over the guy who was bleeding in the street. The second cop, who had been in the front seat, rushed out. I heard her say, "What did you do, Carlos?" Then they messed around in the dark for a long time. Finally, more cops showed up and they took me away. It didn't look right, that's all I know.*

There had been an internal investigation by the police department and the district attorney's office. The newspapers had a great time quoting the criminals, who had no problem slamming Dad and the police in general. Jackson's story, told from his hospital bed, was that he had been walking home after a night of partying when he stumbled on Dad's police cruiser. He admitted that he had been drinking but denied that he had done anything to provoke the cops. *That one pig, the Mexican, he shot me like I was a sick dog. Any soulful man he saw that night was gonna get shot, and that turned out to be me. I want him to pay. Someone has to pay for what happened to me.*

The Elvin Heights Echo had a photograph of Jackson in his hospital bed, a bandage wrapped around his head. The caption read: *Fred Jackson, aka Cold Play: Innocent victim of police shooting?*

I had to laugh. Cold Play had never been innocent of anything. He was one of those white guys who tried to act ghetto, gangsta bullshit. We thought he was stupid. And his nickname was another joke. The guy probably didn't know that he had named himself after a white music group—music that he would never listen to. But then I guess a guy who needs to give himself a handle didn't give a damn about what I thought.

They put Dad on administrative leave while the investigation dragged on. Dad kept telling us that it would be straightened out, that the investigation would go nowhere, but even he admitted that the Department wanted no more of him. My Dad had a reputation for being an aggressive cop; quick to retaliate and much too likely to draw his weapon. He had been involved in two other shootings, and he was the subject of a half-dozen citizen complaints for excessive force. Each time he had been cleared by the Police Review Board, but the complaints stayed in his personnel file. Dad didn't know what to do when he wasn't being a cop, and it showed. One day he told us he was quitting the force. That was when the real trouble started between Dad and Mom.

My cell rang and vibrated.

"What?"

"You cool down?" Jamey asked. We hadn't talked since I had shoved him off our table.

"I'm okay. You?"

"I'm not the one been screwed up. Your old man home yet?"

"He's been around but I haven't seen him. Now Mom's gone, too."

"You're on your own?"

"Nothing new. Look, I'm beat. I need some sleep."

"Let's get together tomorrow, okay?"

"If you want."

"Yeah. Terry told me to act right. Like you're under pressure or something. 'Poor baby,' I said."

"Screw you."

"Yeah, right. We'll hook up tomorrow."

"Later, dude. Easy."

Terry was his on-again, off-again girlfriend. She had more common sense in her pudgy little finger than Jamey had in his whole family.

I sat in the dark for a few more minutes. Eventually I shuffled to my room and flopped on the bed.

About an hour later I threw a few clothes and candy bars into a backpack. I picked up my cell, slipped a cap on my head. I locked all the windows and doors. I snared cash from the envelope I had taped under my bed (about $500 saved from my part-time gig as a busboy) and I wrote a note that said, *I'll be back in a few days. I need to get my head together. Don't worry. I'll be okay*. I signed it "Miguel." I stepped out the door and walked up the street, and it was as though I saw the houses and lawns and driveways for the first time. I looked back at the house and realized that it looked like every other house on the block. I kept on walking even though I didn't know where I was going.

I had to wait forever but eventually I caught the bus at the corner of Wilder and Fortieth. It took me downtown, which seemed as good a place as any to spend the night. I seriously thought about staying on the bus until it got to the edge of El-town, out near the old airport. But then what?

As I debated my short-term future, my cell rang. It was the old man.

"Yeah?" I said. "I wasn't expecting to hear from you."

"Mike. Where are you?"

"I'm on my way to Jamey's. We got some math homework. He always needs my help with that stuff. Where are you?"

"I'm at work. Overtime, under the lights. I had to take a construction job. An old friend put in a good word for me with the foreman and the union. They need a lot of men to get the new courthouse back on schedule. It's crazy out here. Ironic, me working on a courthouse, huh?"

"I guess."

"I can't talk too much, Mike. So you gotta listen good. You and your mother have to be careful. Sandra let me know that Cold Play put a target on my back. I can handle that, but I'm worried about your mother, and you."

I wanted to say that if he had never left, maybe he wouldn't have to worry so much.

"Mom's at Grandma's for a few days. I'll call her and let her know. She won't take your calls."

"I know. I know. What about you?"

"I'm good, Dad. Jamey and me been in tight spots before. This is just Cold Play doin' it macho for his suck-ups. No sweat, Dad. Seriously."

"Yeah, I know, you're a tough guy. But this Cold Play is just enough of an idiot to try to do something. You should be okay at school tomorrow. I'll pick you up after and give you a ride home. About 3:30?"

"No way. I'm not in middle school. I can deal with it. I'll be with Jamey. I'll walk home the long way, by his house. We'll be careful. I thought you had to work, anyway?"

"Yeah, I do. I probably can't get to the school until 4:30. Wait for me, inside. I mean it, Mike."

"I said I'd be okay. I can take care of myself."

"This is serious, Mike. This guy is crazy. He tried to kill me once, that's why I had to shoot him. And he won't let it go. Now that I think about it, I'm going to pick you up in the morning and take you to school. I'll be there by seven-thirty."

I shut the cell. I didn't answer it when he called back.

I called Grandma's number but no one picked up. I texted Mom: *Dad sd b careful. Cold Play threats. Stay @ Grandma a few days*. I didn't mention that I had run away.

I patted my backpack and felt the gun. Jamey and I had bought it a long time before, when we thought that we needed extra protection from the Cutters. I never had to use it, but I figured that it would be a good thing to have as I walked the streets when I . . . well, I wasn't sure what I was trying to do, I only knew that I had to get out of the house and away from everyone and everything. I needed a change, and I was doing the only thing that might cause that change.

* * *

That night was rough. I roamed the streets, confused, sneaking around like a thief, heading for cover whenever I saw headlights. I avoided everyone—the homeless guys, the hookers, the other runaways. Dad's message had put a little panic in my head. Maybe Cold Play was looking for me. What if he found me? What would I do? I decided to leave town, hit the road.

I crashed not too far from the Main Street Mall, down a flight of stairs that led to the small shop where Downtown Barbers had been for years, below street level. I leaned against the door and tried to get comfortable. I had to move broken glass and old newspapers. I made sure no one could see me from the street. I cleaned the area as best I could.

That's when it hit me. What the hell was I doing? I had a warm bed at my house. Food. Cable. I should be going to school in the morning, spending time with Jamey and maybe talking to Andrea, if she would only give me a chance. What did I expect to accomplish scrunched up in a ball hidden away like a bum, a gun pressing against my ribs? Or on the run like an orphan? Did I think I could fix everything on my own? Take care of Cold Play? Get Dad's job back? Get Mom and Dad back together?

The wind picked up. It whistled across the deserted streets, pushing trash and dirt into my concrete cave. I shivered, occasionally drifted off. The night dragged on. I nearly jumped out of my shoes when my cell buzzed. Jamey. The screen flashed 5:38 AM.

"Mike? I'm in a jam. You got to come."

"What is it? What the hell . . . "

"Cold Play grabbed me when I left Terry's last night. He said he couldn't find you, so he settled for me." It almost sounded like Jamey laughed at his own words. "He finally got me to call you. He says you have to do something."

"What does he want? Are you okay?"

He waited a few seconds. He shouted, "Call the cops, your dad! Don't come . . . "

I heard what must have been Jamey getting punched and a loud "Oh!" Then it sounded like the phone had been dropped. A gruff, almost hoarse voice said, "Kid … If you want to see your buddy again, you better listen good. It's your old man. You get him to come and talk to me, and your pal walks out of here okay. If Reséndez ain't here in another hour, Jamey's dead. And you're next."

"What? What do you mean?"

"Don't be stupid, kid. Get your old man here to the football field, at the high school. One hour, six-thirty. You get him here. And tell him he better be alone or this punk is dead, and then you. I know where you and your old lady live." He hung up.

I immediately punched in number 1, Dad's speed dial. He answered on the first ring. I guess he wasn't sleeping either. I tried to explain what was going on, but all I could get out was a jumbled mix of crying and half-sentences.

He finally had to shout at me, "Miguel! Get it together! Goddammit! What is going on?"

It took longer than I wanted but I managed to convince Dad that Jamey was in trouble and needed his help.

"You stay where you are. I'll send Sandra for you and I'll go meet Jackson. I'm gonna bust his ass for good."

"How can you do that?" I was so mixed up that it sounded like Dad was talking as though he was still a cop. He just couldn't give it up.

"I can't explain now, Mike. I've got to get to the football field. Jamey's in real danger. I hope I'm not too late. Wait for Sandra."

My stomach tightened and dry heaves jerked my upper body. I couldn't think straight for a long time. I sweated and shivered, imagined terrible things about Jamey, my Dad and Cold Play. Confusion mixed up with the wind that whipped around me. *I should do what Dad said*, I thought. *But, I can't let Jamey down. It's all my fault.*

That stuff went on in my head until I finally settled down and figured out what I needed to do. I grabbed the gun, stuck it in my pants, made sure I had my money and then I ran up the stairs from my hiding place. I left everything else for the barbers. I tore down windy Main Street heading for the high school and the football field. The gun hindered my running so I pulled it from my pants and held it while I ran. If anyone saw me, they'd have to call the police—crazy teenager running through the dark with a gun.

There was no traffic but some lights had been turned on in a few of the stores and buildings. I heard Jamey's voice as I ran—worried but still telling me to stay away, to let my Dad handle it. Jamey had been willing to get hurt, maybe killed just to keep me out of danger. I saw a bike leaning against a tree in a yard. I didn't slow down as I approached the short picket fence. I jumped over the fence, grabbed the bike, ran it to the gate and took off. A dog jumped at me from behind but I left him barking and howling.

The football field appeared in the night like a giant sleeping black bear. A wire and plywood fence surrounded the field, and the gate was chained and locked up. But I didn't have a problem getting in. The fence had more holes than Grandma Herrera's old aprons, and it was no big deal to get inside to the asphalt strip that circled the field. I left the bike at the fence, found a break in the old wire and crawled in and stayed low, looking for any sign of Dad, Jamey or Cold Play.

When I saw them, I stopped breathing for a few seconds. They were in the end zone under the scoreboard, the darkest place on the field, maybe thirty yards from me. Cold Play must have thought he would be safe there, and the truth was that no one could see him from the street, outside the fence. Dad knelt on the ground, his hands behind his head. Jamey was also on the ground but he was lying down, and I didn't see him move. Cold Play strutted around them, holding a gun pointed at Dad's head. I moved to them, on hands and knees. I thought I inched along slow, so as not to make noise, but in just a few seconds I was close enough that I could hear Cold Play cussing and threatening my father.

"You thought you could burn Cold Play and that'd be it? You dumb pig. Get ready to kiss your ass goodbye, Reséndez. Tonight you pay for messing with me."

"I already said I'm sorry that happened. We can do business together, man. I know stuff that you can use, and I want in on the action. Don't you understand?"

Cold Play swung the gun at Dad and hit him on the jaw. Dad dropped to the grass, next to Jamey. Cold Play held his gun with both hands and aimed at Dad.

I stood up and waved at Cold Play. "Hey, asshole. Over here, you dumb sonofabitch."

I jumped up and down. He stumbled backwards, surprised I guess. Dad screamed something I couldn't understand. Cold Play aimed the gun at me and before I could do anything, he shot at me. The bullet landed a few feet to my right. I hollered although I didn't even think about it. It just came out. I rolled to my left and dug into the ground. I aimed my gun in the general direction of Cold Play.

Dad's rules rolled through my head. *Stop. Look. Be careful. Be aware.* It was too dark and I couldn't take the chance that I might shoot Dad or Jamey. I couldn't see Cold Play anyway. I rolled some more and picked up my head to take another look. I saw no one. I waited a few minutes. Nothing moved except the tips of the grass in the remaining breeze from the windy night. A piece of paper floated across the field and jammed itself against the fence, where it quivered like something dying.

I started to crawl to the end zone, slowly and quietly, and had gone only a few yards when I heard the footsteps behind me. Then I felt the gun at the back of my head.

"What a night for old Cold Play. A trifecta. The pig, his kid and another kid just for grins. Yeah, a great night."

I smelled booze and a sickly, sweet odor of something else coming from Cold Play. It's strange, but I didn't feel afraid. That might sound like bragging but I'm just saying that right then, when Cold Play had his gun pressed against my skull and I waited for the final flash or whatever it was that would happen when he pulled the trigger, right then, I could see clearly, make out details in the dark; I could hear each sound in the night, any little bit of noise, even the beating of Cold Play's crazy heart. And I knew I could handle it. My only thought was that I still needed to do something to help Dad and Jamey. I hadn't finished and I hadn't helped, and that bothered me.

The shot sounded like every movie gun blast I had ever heard, like every explosion in Grand Theft Auto, like every argument Mom and Dad made me sit through. I collapsed on the ground, heaving and breathing deeply but feeling like my lungs were blocked off. Cold Play fell next to me, blood flowing from his mouth, a gurgling noise coming out of his nose, tiny red bubbles covering his lips.

Dad reached down and picked me up. He hugged me, and I think we were both crying.

"How . . . ?" I stammered.

"The dummy didn't think that I might have a back up. Hidden in my boot. I was waiting for my chance. You gave it to me, Mike."

"Jamey?" I said.

"He's hurt, beat up pretty bad. But he'll be all right."

I looked over Dad's shoulder. The sun was coming up over the downtown buildings. A half-dozen cops were running into the field. Four of them surrounded us, two checked out Cold Play. Sandra stepped forward.

"Carlos, you all right? I told you to wait for backup. ¡*Cabezón!*" She slugged him on the shoulder, then she smiled. "Your boy, he okay?"

An ambulance raced onto the field and Jamey was loaded aboard and then hauled away. Sandra called his parents.

There were more questions but I didn't say too much. Dad had to tell the story of what happened at least three times to different cops and detectives. It looked like the cops didn't know how to deal with Dad. At least there wasn't a question about it being self-defense. Finally, they let him take me home. Sandra said she would make sure the bike I had "borrowed" would be returned. She grabbed my gun, too.

Dad took me to the motel where he was sleeping. He could tell that I was tired, completely beat, so he didn't ask me any more questions or dig into what I was doing on the street, with a gun, or what the hell did I think I was doing at the football field. He saved all that for the next day. When he was finished with me, he called Mom and told her what had happened. Dad and I talked a lot waiting for Mom. I think he needed that. Then she picked me up and took me home where I had to deal with another lecture, then more crying from her, and finally hugs and kisses.

A few days later, Jamey and I were able to talk without anyone else around.

"So, your Dad is still a cop, undercover, eh? That's wild—crazy but cool, know what I mean?"

"Yeah, I know exactly what you mean. He said not to tell anyone, not even you."

"You serious? You know you can trust me. Who else you got?"

"Yeah. It's all good. I think he expects me to tell you."

"There you go."

"Anyway, Dad and Sandra had been trying to stop the burglary ring for months. Cold Play and that Zebra guy are just part of the gang. The burglaries are a small piece of what they're in to. When Dad had to shoot Cold Play it gave him an idea, an excuse to put himself on the street in civilian clothes. A way to get inside the gang."

"But they didn't find a gun. The story was that Cold Play didn't have a weapon."

"Dad explained that. When Cold Play got shot he managed to kick his gun down the sewer drain, and Dad and Sandra acted like they couldn't find it. Dad's trying to make contact with one of the leaders of the gang, someone who doesn't think much of Cold Play. Dad said his own rep is shot now, and everyone thinks he's dirty. That's how he wanted it."

"He should have told you, or your Mom at least."

"He thought it was too dangerous for us to know. But it didn't matter anyway. Cold Play made his move."

"Your Dad stopped him. Ain't his cover blown?"

"Maybe. Maybe not. Since Cold Play is dead, there's only a few who know the real story. You for one."

Jamey tried to smile but he looked nervous.

"Dad shooting Cold Play gives him some cred with the gang. Cold Play wasn't too popular. That's why you can't say anything, Jamey. *Nada*."

He extended his hand and we knuckle-bumped. Jamey would never tell anyone.

"But your mom and dad are over? This didn't fix it?"

"No way. If anything, she hates him worse now. He almost got me killed, according to her. I've tried to tell her it wasn't his fault. He saved me. But that's not the way she looks at it."

Jamey nodded.

"When you get those stitches out?" I asked. "They are ugly, bro. How can Terry stand to kiss that face?"

"Hey, man. She's all over me now, like syrup on a pancake. Nothing better than a good beating so women will act nice and accommodating. Too bad nothing happened to you that you can use on Andrea. You missed your chance. You should have got wounded, or something. At least."

"Yeah, too bad. Maybe next time."

THE SMELL OF ONIONS

Shorty stumbled from the Rainbow Inn
Jenny would give him hell
again

no patience for her father
these days

where's that damn car?

tight legs
the arthritis had him gnarled
like a piñón tree

too old to hang with punks
what do they know
about playing pool?

back in '63
they played real pool
on the Westside

Snipe
Porfy
Dutch Borman
man he was tough
had to be to drink
with pachucos
mojados from Juárez
locos from L.A.
and then
kick their ass at pool

he wiped his nose
with the back of his skinny
gray-haired wrist
that once had the touch
that could win hundreds
in one night

no one believed him
but he remembered
when his stroke was clean and quick

crip
wino
bum
begging a few bucks
for T-Bird
betting on rounds of pool
for Jenny and the rent
his legs kept him up
half the night

reefer helped
when he could get it

one day
he would pack it in
back to the Valley
where he could
die in the sun
stretched out in a field
the smell of onions in the air
chicharras buzzing the hot midday

bony fingers grabbed him
by the neck
twisted him to the curb

you forgot
yesterday was payday
viejo?
you play Humberto?
that's stupid
viejo
I don't like stupid

Hummy kicked
wheezing lungs could not explain
a little more time
his check was late
the *pendejo* mailman

the street light caught a silvery gleam
clean and quick

hey, man, you don't know
I should be in the Valley
in a field smelling onions

this ain't the goddamned Valley
this ain't the Valley

LOVERS

THE SCENT OF TERRIFIED ANIMALS

"I hate the mountains." Her back rested against a faded, splintered corral fence.

The smell of burning pine clung to the tourist ranch. Smoke floated across the sky, hiding the scenery and corrupting the air.

Irritation slipped into his voice. "How can you say that? You told me you loved the outdoors, hiking. Christ! If I'd known . . . if you had said anything before . . . damn, we could have gone to L.A., Vegas, any place. You hate the mountains? Good God, you hate the mountains!" He stepped back from her and rushed away to their cabin.

She could only stare after him. She should have said something. That was easy to see. She should have told him many things and she wondered when she would. The bank, her friends, the party, the wedding—it all happened so fast and, she had to admit, she had been swept up in the flow of events and the energy of her office romance—the famous affair. She could not resist Philip. And now she was in the mountains, surrounded by smoke and fire, and she had no idea what she was doing.

The ranch's owner invited them to his cabin for drinks the night they were the last remaining guests. They sat on rickety wooden chairs the old man spread among the weeds and cacti.

"This is a shame, folks, what with you on your honeymoon and all. 'Course, young people like you got a lot of other things to do 'sides hiking around these hills, eh?" He chuckled, amused with his brashness.

Mary and Philip ignored his remark.

He shrugged and poured more drinks. "The forest won't recover, least not for me to ever see it. Have to pack it in, try to sell. Don't see how, though, not with the park burned out."

Philip said, "I had hoped we could come back next year, but I guess there won't be much to see. Not much point."

Mary groaned. "Oh, Philip. Don't be an idiot. Of course there won't be much around here, the whole damn place is burning down! Can't you see what's happening? Can't you smell it?"

Calhoun clucked his teeth. He waited for the man to respond.

Mary kept at it. "There might be some fish in the ranch pond. They're put there every year just for the tourists—right, Calhoun? You said you always wanted to catch a fish, Philip. Won't your man, what's his name . . . ?"

Calhoun answered, "Montoya."

"Yes. Montoya. Won't he stock up your little lake so that Philip can catch his fish? You can do that next year, even without trees, without anything else around here. Just you and your fish, Philip, you and your fish." She presented her empty glass to Calhoun and he filled it with whiskey.

The smoke carried the scent of terrified animals. The fire's dull roar served as background for all other sounds. They sat without speaking, drinking, watching the moon appear for a few minutes and then succumb to the smoke. The mountains were dim, weak silhouettes.

The old man stretched. "This is the worst one I've ever seen, and I've been in mountains and woods and forests most of my sixty years. A stupid tourist did this. What a waste." He might have been giving a tour of the ranch, pointing out the sights.

Mary tilted her glass to her lips and the liquor rolled down her throat. "Yes, Calhoun, a waste—a lousy, goddamned waste. Good night. I'm going to bed. Philip?"

"Go ahead. Don't wait up."

She stood and knocked back her chair, and it lay on its side in the dirt.

"I apologize for my wife, Mr. Calhoun. The fire ruined the trip for us. She needs to do something. She gets bored easily. Women? What can you do? Guess we'll go on into the city. She'll be all right as soon as we get away from the smoke."

Many years earlier Calhoun would have told Philip what he thought. But now he was a good businessman and he offered Philip only more whiskey.

They finished the bottle and started a second one. It was too much for Philip. He passed out and Calhoun left him slumped in his chair. His thin jacket flapped with the night wind. His hair and skin soaked up the smoke. Mary did not come looking for him.

***

Calhoun sat on the steps to his cabin. The hazy, gray sky had slowed him and he slept later than usual. His throat was parched from the smoky air that surrounded his land. He heard Mary and Philip shouting at each other until one of them slammed against the cabin's wall.

Philip ran out. For a minute he stood motionless, undecided about his next act, lost as surely as if he had been dropped from the sky into the most desolate area of the park. He saw the crude, hand-painted sign with the word "Fishing" hanging over the shed where Montoya drank coffee and read the newspaper.

"I want to fish. I'll rent equipment, buy a can of worms. Whatever I need."

Montoya had been taught by Calhoun to overlook the quirks of the tourists. He needed the job and he learned quickly. He grunted in the direction of Philip. "Any fish you catch will cost you a dollar an inch."

Mary strode from the cabin a half hour later, her eyes musky and red, her skin as clouded as the smoke-ringed sun. She wore shorts and a halter top in the coolness of the overcast day. She stood near the corral and watched the horses.

* * *

The breeze picked up dust from the corral and blew it across her face and into her eyes. She closed her eyes suddenly and hard, to make them water, but the dirt did not flow out. She frantically rubbed her eyes, her face, the skin on her arms. She was caught in the panic of the dust.

A rough hand grabbed her. She smelled the horses. The hand pulled her fingers away from her face.

"Here, let me help. You could scratch an eyeball, rubbing like that." He held her face and she was locked in his grip. He said, "Open your eyes, slowly. I'll hold your eyelid open, you move your eye, slowly, up and down, side to side."

He held her thin eyelid with the tips of his fingers. The delicate touch surprised her. She followed his instructions and the dirt moved then fell out of her eye. Her eyes watered and tears flowed down her face.

"That was horrible. Thanks." She twisted her face away from him and he dropped his hands, awkwardly, away from her body.

She was almost as tall as him. His black eyes and hair blended with the sunburnt darkness of his skin, and she thought he was nearly as dark as the Puerto Rican teller who helped her close up the bank.

"It'll be sore for a few minutes. You'll be okay."

She heard a difference in his Mexican accent from the teller's. Slower, she thought.

"I'd like to go for a ride on one of your animals, if you're letting the horses out."

"I can give you one of the older ones, but you can't go far. The horses are spooked by the smoke. They won't go in the direction of the fire. They smell the smoke, hear it burning. Around the ranch, on the path, that's fine."

She nodded agreement.

He climbed the fence and jumped into the corral. He inched his way to the four horses huddled against the far end and talked gently and softly to them. They were unsure. The year was too young for the gray sky. They shied away from Montoya and he had trouble catching one. He lunged at them until he managed to grab a tail. He patted the horse and rubbed her flanks to calm her.

Mary watched him ready the horse. He was steady and deliberate. The horse grudgingly permitted the saddle and bridle. Montoya led the horse out of the gate.

"Lady will take you around the ranch. She could do it blindfolded. Just let her have her way. Don't make her run, she's too old, and she doesn't like kicks or shouts. You'll have an easy ride." He handed the reins to Mary.

"Won't you ride, too? I could use the company." She climbed on the saddle.

"No. Calhoun's rules. When you're back, find me and I'll cool her down and put her with the others. I'll be around." He slapped the neck of the horse to start her trotting along the deeply rutted path.

***

Philip had caught more than a dozen fish. The overstocked pond rippled with fish as they struggled for food. His catch lay twisted on the shore, a cord strung through their gills, their bodies half covered with water. The bundle of fish squirmed in the water as they slowly died.

Mary rode by on the plodding horse. She didn't look at him. He waved at her and pointed at his fish and started to lift them for her to see but she rode over the small rise that separated the pond from the cabins. She kicked the horse to make her run. Philip threw his line back in the water.

***

Montoya found Lady outside the couple's cabin, saddled and hot, standing alone, her flanks wet with foam. He led her to the corral where he did his best to cool her. Philip strolled up to him, dragging his line of fish, uncleaned, stiff from death.

"Son of a bitch! Man, you got to gut those fish. And that's a hundred bucks, easy, maybe one and a half. Haven't you ever fished?" Before Philip answered, Montoya blurted out, his voice high and tight, "And your wife! She almost killed this horse, running her into the ground, and then leaving her hot. I told her to find me. What's wrong with you?"

Philip's eyes turned away. "She knows about horses. She's been around them. Maybe you better tell her how she screwed up." His words came slowly, wrenched from him with an effort he had trouble finishing. "I'm going to fish again, try for two hundred dollars." He walked back to the pond.

Montoya turned to the horse. He brushed and patted her and listened to Philip walking out of sight. The hired hand finished with the horse and then he returned to the cabin. He stood by the door for a few minutes, opened it and walked in.

From the steps, Calhoun saw all that happened. He did not want to have the talk with Montoya but it was not to be avoided. Montoya had to go. The hired hand didn't understand these people; he had no way of knowing how much trouble she could make for him and what she could do to him in the town where business had swirled into the sky with the smoke from the trees. The only question for Calhoun was whether Montoya would leave the cabin before Philip reappeared.

The smoke billowed over the mountains and rolled into the valley, and Calhoun's eyes stung from the smell of dead, burning earth.

THE 405 IS LOCKED DOWN

When Alberto Ortiz left a message about speaking on the Cal State campus, Tomás reacted in his usual manner.

Never happen.

A few days later the professor's second call caught the writer in his office. "I'm sorry I didn't return your message," Tomás offered. "You know how it is sometimes."

"*Por favor, no se preocupe.* We are all too busy these days. That's what life is like in the twenty-first century, no? Especially for us Latinos." The animated professor had the appropriate respectful tone. "I greatly admire your book, and the few stories I've found that you've published."

"Thank you," the writer said.

"You and your multifaceted book," Ortiz explained as though he was addressing a student, "have been a hot topic in my classes several times. The discourse has been quite lively. Clearly, there were two opposing views about your writing. Finally, the MEChA students suggested that I try to get you on campus to speak. It was their idea but I supported it completely and got the department head to approve."

The professor summarized the high points of his proposal—class lecture, evening book reading and signing at the local bookstore where students and faculty congregated, maybe an interview for the university radio station.

When he finished Tomás tried to be polite. "I appreciate the attention," he said. "But the time away from my writing is too valuable. A trip out-of-state to a college campus has no relevance to putting words down on paper. I've missed one deadline already and spending two or three days in Los Angeles will do nothing for the next chapter in my follow-up book. I'm up against the wire with my editor."

But then Ortiz said, "You're aware that I'm a producer, right? Sure, I teach, have for years. Almost ready to retire. *Pero*, I, uh, we, have a production company, Sueños Unlimited. Me and my partner, Mónica Suárez, we've put together a few projects."

"Is the cliché true then?" Tomás asked. "Everyone in L.A. is in the movie business, waiters to university professors?"

"There are days it looks that way. But this is not a hobby for me. Maybe you saw the documentary on PBS last fall, *A Cultural History of East Los Angeles*? We were part of that and now we want to do something more intense, more substantial. We think that project is your book."

He paused and both men thought about an appropriate reaction to the professor's words.

"Tomás," Ortiz carried on when the writer did not speak, "your visit out here would give us the opportunity to talk to you about our ideas, make the pitch for your book. The time is right. There isn't just a Latin Boom going on—it's a damn explosion. Music, art, the Internet. J-Lo and Smits still riding high long after they should have burned out. So many Latinos getting attention now. I want to make sure we, the Mexican Americans, get our share. *¿Cómo no?* We are taking over. There's no doubt. A movie can be big now. Your book has great audience potential, and that translates as great market numbers."

"It's nice of you to say that about my book. But you actually think there's a movie in it? I'm not sure it's all that visual."

The words came smoothly, as though without effort, but the writer's guts swirled, his tongue felt thick, his heart pumped ambition. A movie, even a small one, could set him up, he thought. Give him the cushion he needed to devote full time to writing. Screw that deadline.

"That's what a good producer can do, Tomás." The professor's earnestness crackled through the phone. "And we, Sueños Unlimited, are good. We get the experts involved to make sure that the film that comes from your book not only does justice to the book but gives a movie audience what it wants. You should come out here so we can talk about that kind of detail. You interested?"

Yeah, he was interested.

They worked out dates, travel arrangements, book orders. The professor sent the writer a university standard contract, a form for the IRS and a map of the campus with the Chicano Studies building circled in red. Then Tomás waited until the day came for him to begin the adventure that would make his name a household word. And a nice wad of cash.

Outside the terminal the smog and heat greeted Tomás with enthusiasm. He shuddered from LAX chaos and almost immediately a dead weight of doubt settled on his back. He had abandoned the dry, warm, healthier air of Denver and flown into hot Los Angeles for no better reason than the slim chance for some big money. He suspected that too many other people had fled to L.A. for the same reason and that West Coast reality had a lousy way of smashing fantasies and dreams. At least he had a time limit on his hunt for the golden pot at the end of the City of Angels rainbow. Three days and he would be gone.

Ninety minutes later Tomás was on the telephone talking with Professor Ortiz again.

"It's great you could make it for the students," Ortiz said with no hint of sarcasm. The professor and the writer both understood that talking to the professor's Post-Chicano Chicano Literature class served to cover the writer's expenses and a token honorarium. It was not the reason for the trip.

"Glad to do it, Alberto," Tomás said. "I owe you for using my book in your classes. Maybe the students can help me with ideas for the next one."

"Oh yeah. You bet." Ortiz cleared his throat. "Some of them can't wait to talk to you." A slight pause, then he said, "Mónica will meet us for dinner tonight, I'll pick you up in about twenty minutes. We can talk about the class, and the deal, of course. We are both excited about this."

The deal.

The food at the restaurant represented at least four different cultures, and the ambience of the place was cool, hip, so Californian. Tomás ate and drank too much and did not worry about it because he was not paying. He watched his hosts get a bit sloppy on wine and then blue margaritas. Long after the dessert plates had been cleared, a full carafe of the vile concoction sat next to a pair of empty carafes. Clumps of soggy salt and twisted lemon rinds littered the tablecloth.

Ortiz dominated the conversation with tales of various actors and actresses whose paths he had crossed, with remembrances of past film and theater projects that had almost broken through, with references to friends in the business who owed him favors. He gravitated to an older generation of actors—Tony Plana, Elizabeth Peña, Cheech Marin. At one point he said, "Tony would be great for this project. And he's got the smarts to recognize that this is bound to hit big. I'll see if we can meet with him before you leave town."

Mónica Suárez was about ten years younger than Ortiz and ten steps ahead of him on everything connected to their business. The writer could not gauge the level of their personal involvement, or even if there was any.

The evening stretched on and Tomás started to worry about the professor's inebriation.

When Mónica had a chance she turned the conversation to Tomás' book. "The way it speaks to young Chicanos is so true," she said, leaving the writer thinking about what a false-speaking book might be. "Your writing's not about the new surge of undocumenteds or the old Movement heavies or the slick Hispanic politicians of the Nineties. None of that six-hundred-page family saga from Old Mexico to the barrios of urban America. No spiritualism or *bruja* mythology. Just straight to the hearts and minds of young Latinos, the ones listening to hip-hop and reggaeton. Realism about growing up in this country when your own family is confused about who they are, when you yourself can't figure it out, you can't define your own culture, whether it's that neither the music of José Alfredo Jiménez or Los Lobos relates to you, or that Aztlán sounds quaint and old-fashioned, or that you can't distinguish between Corky Gonzales and José Angel Gutiérrez and you don't even care that you can't."

"Whoa." The writer held up his hand. "You can take my book however you want. What readers get is not always what I intended."

"There I go again. Sometimes I say too much, too quickly. I have to, to get a word in with him."

The professor fidgeted in his chair. He clinked glasses together, dropped his napkin on the floor and made a production out of retrieving it. His hands did not stop moving. Finally, he blurted, "Tomás, you will have a good, good crowd tomorrow night." His voice was a decibel too loud. "Your signing has attracted a lot of attention. It'll be a late night. *Una noche maravillosa.*"

Mónica groaned. "You don't need any more late nights," she said. "And I can't take any more with you."

"And if you don' make it, so wha'?" the professor growled.

"You can flirt with your students without looking over your shoulder, that's what."

"You're embarrassin' me and yourself. Have some respect for Tomás."

"Keep the dirt to myself, is that it?" Mónica turned to Tomás. "Have I embarrassed us? Or you?"

"I'm only concerned about tomorrow," Tomás said. For a second he considered saying something about watching an Albee play. "Is everything okay? Anything I need to do to help?"

"What you mean," she said, "is will this *borracho* be in any shape tomorrow to pull this off? What do you think, Alberto? You going to be too hungover?"

"Don' worry 'bout me." The professor's head tilted downward and he spoke to a stain on the floor. "I'll be ready. And so will my students."

He stood up awkwardly and excused himself. He muttered something about the *baño*.

Tomás finished his drink and assumed that the evening was over. He needed a good night's sleep.

"Alberto won't be able to drive," Mónica said. "He's never handled his liquor well, especially tequila." She squinted at him over the salty rim of her drink. What he could see of her pupils glistened. The writer attributed both effects to the syrupy drinks. "He drank much more tonight than he's used to. He must have been trying to impress you."

"I didn't think he drank that much."

"Lately," Mónica said, slightly slurring the words, "when we go out we usually end up calling a cab, or bumming a ride. Some mornings we can't remember where we left our cars."

"You surprise me," he said. "I have to rely on you. If he can't function tomorrow, where does that leave me? Why bring me out here just for this? "

Mónica looked away. She said, "I'm sorry. But I think he will be all right. He does recover remarkably well, as long as he gets enough sleep." She sipped her drink. "We're such bad hosts, and you, the guest without a car or friend in this city. *Qué mal educados somos.*"

"I'm a bit tight myself," Tomás said. "But I'll drive if you think that would be better than either of you. You will have to tell me where to go. I have no idea where I am or how to get back to the hotel. Alberto picked me up and I didn't pay attention to landmarks or street signs."

The squinting had increased and Tomás thought she had closed her eyes altogether. She asked, "What time do you have to be on campus?"

"Alberto said that he would have someone at my place around nine forty-five to make it to his office by ten thirty for the eleven o'clock class. Then I stay on campus for the rest of the day, meeting with different student groups and some faculty. Hang around until the book signing at the bookstore. I guess eating is somewhere in the plan."

She tried to laugh but it did not quite happen. "He's not a detail guy. At least he thought about getting you to campus in time for the class."

Alberto appeared at the side of the table. He wobbled. His hair was wet and the front of his shirt looked damp. His eyes refused to focus on Mónica or Tomás.

"God, you've gotten drunker," Mónica said. "We should go, Alberto. We have to get Tomás back to his hotel."

Ortiz fell to his knees. The writer looked at Mónica for direction, but all he got was her disgust. Tomás grabbed the professor under the arms and tried to help him stand. Ortiz jerked away. "Le' me go!" he blurted.

Tomás released Ortiz and moved away from him. Other customers were staring, some laughed nervously, some glared.

The professor's shirttail hung outside his pants and the laces of his right shoe were untied. Spit dribbled from his lips. "Mónica, I . . . I." He slumped forward.

Tomás reached for him but he was too slow. The professor's hand desperately clutched the tablecloth. Glasses, silverware, carafes and blue liquor tumbled from the table and crashed on the restaurant's colorful tiled floor.

Mónica jumped to her feet. "*¡Bruto!*" she screamed. "I've had it!"

She turned and bumped a waiter who had rushed to help. He fell against a woman waiting for her plate of food to cool. The plate and the food landed in the woman's lap. Mónica stumbled out of the restaurant.

The writer had to use his credit card to pay the four hundred dollars demanded by the restaurant manager.

Tomás propped the professor against the side wall of the restaurant until the taxi arrived. He squeezed Ortiz into the back seat, then climbed in next to the professor and shouted the name of his hotel to the cabdriver.

"That's gonna be tough tonight," the cabbie drawled. His black skin absorbed the light from the restaurant's entrance.

The writer could see the driver's eyes but not any specifics of his face. "God, now what?"

The driver said, "Your bad luck. The 405's locked down. A high-speed chase on the freeway—dozens of cops and one suicidal white man from up north. But the real problem is that the chase caused several accidents includin' one where a semi jackknifed. Son-of-a-gun blew up. Must've been carryin' some nasty shit. You could see the fireball over in Long Beach. Traffic's stopped for miles. Your hotel's really not that far away, but gettin' there is gonna be a bitch. I'll have to go around, use the 10 or the 110, maybe some of the side streets. It's a ripple effect when this sort of thing happens. Everythin' gets messed up. Sorry, pal, but this could be an expensive ride."

Tomás shook his head. "Never mind. Take this guy over to Cal State, L.A. This is a map of the building where his office is. You can leave him there—a security guard or someone like that will take him in. I don't care what you do with him." The cabbie's face turned even darker when he frowned. "They know him over there," Tomás quickly added. "He's one of their professors. He'll be okay. Here's seventy-five bucks for your trouble. It's all I got."

The cabbie hesitated and did not accept the money. "Gee, pal, that's dicey. It's late to be drivin' around the campus." He stared at the writer. "And what you gonna do?"

The men were bathed in bright white from headlights. Mónica stuck her head out the window of her car and hollered, "Tomás! Come on! Bring that asshole with you."

Tomás stuffed all of his bills in his pocket except for a twenty, which he handed to the cabdriver. He loaded Alberto into Mónica's car. He paused before he sat in the front seat but he did not have an option. He listened to her furious condemnation of Alberto on the way back to the hotel. She drove through the residential streets with practiced precision but more speed than Tomás wanted. She avoided the freeways and had Tomás at his hotel in less than a half-hour.

Somewhere during the ride, Alberto woke up. He mumbled incoherently. He tried to apologize but he could not finish a sentence. He passed out again.

"I'm not driving him anywhere," Mónica said when she had parked the car in the hotel lot. "Take him with you, let him sleep it off in your room."

"You think that's a good idea?"

"It's the only idea. I'll help you."

They struggled with Alberto through the parking lot and hotel lobby. In the elevator, Tomás said, "That booze hit him hard. He shouldn't drink if this is the result. Getting drunk I might understand, but he's practically comatose."

"It's not just the alcohol," Mónica said.

They lifted Alberto and dragged and pushed him to the room. They dumped him on the floor. Mónica sat on a chair and Tomás sat on the bed.

"Why did you say it's not the alcohol?"

"It's everything." She slumped in the chair. "Maybe I don't know what it really is. Being in the film business is so important to him. And his medicines. That started with his bike accident and the broken leg. He denies it but he can't stay away from the damn pills. And I think his so-called energy shake makes it worse. Who knows what's in that? He makes a new batch every morning, as if it was doing him some good."

Tomás rubbed his eyes.

"If he drinks," Mónica continued, "this is what can happen. And sometimes it does happen, although tonight has been the worst."

"Why in the hell does he drink then?" he asked.

"Why does he do stupid things? Why can't he grow up? When will he stop his *pendejadas*, his flings and personal disasters? I can't answer those questions. Believe me, I've asked them."

She shoved her face in her hands and cried. Hard sobs shook her shoulders and neck.

He escaped into the bathroom and stayed there until he heard her moving around. He flushed the toilet, rinsed his hands, threw water on his face and walked back in the room.

"I feel like an idiot," she said to him as soon as he appeared. "You must think we're crazy. I don't blame you. We are nuts."

He knew that he should tell her that it was all right, that everyone has a bad night once in a while, that tomorrow they would laugh about it.

"I need to get some sleep," he said.

"Yes, of course," she said, nodding. "You have to be ready for all the students and fans."

Tomás shrugged. "This movie talk. Was that all it was? Just talk?"

"No, no. We need some time. And money, of course. Getting you on board gives us the talking point we need for the people who have to back this type of project. But it takes time. It always does. We will be another step closer after tomorrow. With the right luck we can do something important. It's all about luck out here."

She picked up her purse. She paused at the doorway.

"I could stay," she said. "He's out cold, dead. I can leave early in the morning. He'll never know."

"You should go."

She left.

Alberto's snores filled the room. Tomás slept fitfully and finally at five in the morning he gave up. He called the front desk and asked for a taxi.

"Certainly, sir, where to?"

"The airport."

"Checking out a day early, sir?"

"No. Someone's here, still using the room. He's paying for the room, so I hope you don't mind."

The desk clerk was all business. "Certainly not, sir. The room is reserved and paid for until tomorrow. As long as you don't break any laws you can do whatever you want."

"Good. And I'll need to talk with someone about changing a flight. You got any coffee?"

THE TRUTH IS

1989

"The truth is, he was a pig." Doris gulped her drink, sucked on her cigarette and tapped blue fingernails on the bar's counter. Carl, the bartender, nodded in agreement and pulled two bills from the stack near her glass. "A filthy, good for nothin', two-timin', blood-suckin' pig."

"Like I said, he was just another customer to me. You two were in here plenty. He never gave me no trouble."

"Yeah, sure. What do you know? You never went home with the guy. You never introduced him to your friends, you never planned nothin' with him, you never, oh hell, you just never."

"Whatever, Doris. I guess I never. You ought to call it a night. It's almost last call anyway."

She tossed most of the money in her purse, checked for her keys and walked out of the bar.

She could hear the telephone ringing through the door to her place. The key wouldn't fit. Her glasses slipped down her nose and she couldn't see. The ringing continued. She dropped her purse and bent over to pick it up, but the floor rushed up to grab her and she fell face first onto the gritty, dusty hall carpet.

"Oh, crap. Where's that key? I'm comin', damn it, I'm comin'. Don't hang up."

She groped for her glasses, found them and twisted them around her ears. On her knees, at eye level with the keyhole, she maneuvered the key into place, turned it and the door swung open. She moved forward, still on her knees, and jerkily made her way to the chair where she normally threw her coat. She used it to help her stand up. The ringing continued.

She rubbed her eyes, tried to clear her brain. She flicked on the light, and her eyes squinted from the glare. She could see the red telephone on the kitchen table where she had left it that morning, after she had carried it to every room in her apartment, dialing the number then pressing the recall button again and again. There had been no answer.

She stood over the ringing machine, her hands shaking. She lit a cigarette, threw the match in the ashtray. The ringing continued. She walked past the table and opened a cupboard. She took out a tall glass, opened the refrigerator, grabbed ice cubes and her bottle of vodka, and made herself a drink. She sat at the table and watched the telephone ring. She sat through the night, drinking and smoking until she fell asleep.

A few nights later Doris and her friend Jodi stumbled into Carl's bar.

"I thought you were all broken up, Doris. Looks like you've recovered."

Jodi said, "The fact is, Carl, she's got better things to do than waste her time over that guy. You think she's gonna sit around, waiting for the phone to ring? He was a pig."

WHY BOSTON IS HIS FAVORITE TOWN

"I met him at the training camp they sent us to. So we would know something about the country before we got there. We had to learn how to act, what we were supposed to say, what local customs we had to be sure not to violate. We spent two weeks at the camp, in Chicago, then off I went to Mexico and he went to Africa. We wrote each other, you know, almost every day."

He could see her diligently putting down on paper the day's events, maybe looking at his picture. He thought a letter from her would have to be funny; she had a weird sense of humor.

She continued. "We got together when our year was up, in Boston. I felt good; he's not like anyone I know. I feel good about us."

She drank from her gin and tonic and he saw her eyes reflected in the neon of the bar's beer signs. He thought she had the most beautiful green eyes he had ever seen. He bought her drinks after work to listen to her talk and to watch her eyes in the smoke of her cigarettes. He liked the feeling of falling in love.

"But did the two of you spend any time alone, together, you know what I mean?"

"Well, sure, there was Boston . . . "

"That was only a week."

"And then I went with him back to Africa for the summer. What do you think, that I don't know him? I know him quite well, if you must ask."

"Africa? What the hell did you do there?" Africa sounded wrong; that would not be where he would take her. Paris or Rio, that's where she belonged.

"Africa was beautiful. We started in the Ivory Coast and ended up in Morocco. I loved it. You can't imagine what it's like, especially the desert, the sun and heat. I've never known anything like that."

He imagined her sweating in the African afternoon, her white linen shirt pasted to her brown skin; her hair, almost blonde from the sun, smeared against her forehead in tiny spirals. He wanted to cool her with ice wrapped in a towel. "Yeah, well that must have been nice, just the two of you, on your own in the wild African wastelands."

"Well, his parents were with us, and my little sister, too. But, yes, that's when we decided to live together. Of course, he had to finish school, he had another year. I came out here to live with my aunt and save some money so we could eventually get a place together in Boston. Working as a Y.M.C.A. counselor in Mexico or Africa doesn't put any money in the bank. It's almost impossible to find an apartment in Boston that's clean and cheap. We had to hire a real estate agent, really, to shop around for us. He says it's nice, close to his job."

"He's in Boston, waiting for you, so off you go next month to set up house. Cozy. What will you do, run the local Y?"

She laughed. "No. That's over. He's got a good job in a publishing company. One of the guys he roomed with at college introduced him to his father, he owns the business, and now he's an assistant editor or something like that. He's great with words, you know. His letters cheer me up. They made me laugh in Mexico. It could be lonely there."

"You speak great Spanish. You must have made friends. I'm sure you weren't alone."

"Oh, sure, I had friends. People at the Y, some of the teachers at the school who taught English. Don't know why I said lonely. It was my first year away from home. I really liked it. It would be nice to go back and teach down there, but he never has liked Mexico, he says. Wants to settle down in Boston. Maybe I can teach there."

"There's Mexicans in Boston, sure, but you got all those Puerto Ricans. Your talents might come in handy."

She was surprised that he thought she had talents. He ordered more drinks.

"I can hardly wait, really. Boston is almost like home, my grandfather was from there and I stayed with him a lot when I was a little girl. He sort of raised me; he died last year. I miss him. I rarely saw my parents after the divorce, so I bounced around from aunt to aunt, and to him, when he had the time. He was very busy, a lawyer who knew Truman and the Kennedys and people like that, but he took me when he could. I miss him."

"You must be rich."

"Not me. Maybe he was, but you wouldn't know it. He was always in a beat up sweater smoking a smelly pipe. Once I asked him why my father never called, and he told me it was up to me to call him or whoever I wanted to talk to. I couldn't wait for the phone to ring. I remembered that in Mexico."

"So you called your boyfriend every day?"

"No. But I wrote every day, even when his letters were late. I didn't wait for the phone to ring, or for mail to be answered." She pulled a cigarette from her purse and he lit it for her. She took a long, deep drag. "I miss the old guy. It would've been nice to have him around now that I'm moving to Boston. He died last year."

There were tears in her beautiful green eyes. They must be for her grandfather, he thought, but he knew that talking with her made him sad and he wished that she would leave for Boston that night, and he hated the idea of falling in love.

HONESTY IS THE BEST POLICY

I didn't love her. I made that clear from the jump. For me it was all about the sex. For her too, when she was honest. That first night, after we left the bar and she asked me to walk her home, we clawed and bit at each other like hungry tigers. We liked it so much I stayed in her apartment for a week. We humped, bumped and jumped in those three rooms without caring what we broke or where we landed. We ordered pizza or noodle bowls when our energy lagged. I lost my job, my room at the motel and the junk I kept there, but we didn't care. We were sexed up and high on lovemaking fumes.

The morning she told me not to come back, I shrugged. "Yeah, sure, whatever." It was all about the sex.

I punched the fence around the corner from her place and broke a finger. When the doc asked me what happened, I said, "Rough sex."

CHICANISMO

LA VISIÓN DE MI MADRE

Florence, Colorado 1956

Tony died in Vietnam when a bullet from a high-powered automatic weapon tore out most of his intestines and stomach. At the instant of death, as his blood flowed into the dark, damp earth of the jungle, the ghost of his grandfather Adolfo walked up to him, cradled his head and murmured something in Spanish. Tony could see the old man smiling, tears in his eyes. The gleam from Adolfo's gold filling reminded Tony how the light from the dining room lamp reflected off the tooth as the old man told the kids his stories of old Mexico, Pancho Villa, gambling with the devil, and, of course, La Llorona.

Tony would sit with a glass of pop, listening to Adolfo. The boy took a drink each time the grandfather sipped his bourbon. Adolfo's voice boomed across the room in a rhapsodic mixture of Spanish and English flowing with poetry, curses, songs and other sounds the children did not understand. They all fit into the story at just the right time.

When Tony was eight he visited the river for the first time with Johnny, his older cousin, and some of Johnny's friends. It was a hot, dry summer with days that stretched for miles across the cloudless sky, yellow and lazy. They swam in a deep, still pool. Trees hid the place from the highway that followed the river for a short span outside the town.

Tony floated for what seemed like hours, forgotten by the other boys. The river was lower than usual, the trees more brittle, but the water was cool.

He thought of his missing mother and the father who was only a shadow standing over him in the night, tall and dark. He wanted to know why they were gone, why she had given him over to the grandparents, and he brooded in the water, unable to shake the feeling of desertion that engulfed him in the sticky heat of summer.

Tony drifted, almost asleep, when he noticed the change. The *chicharras* quit humming. Birds flew from the trees in squawking bunches. Then—silence. Tony opened his eyes but the sun's glare reflected off the water and blinded him.

He swam to the rocks, quickly put on his clothes and shivered. Johnny and his friends were gone. No wind stirred the wild grass. Smothering quiet lay on the river.

"Oh-h-h. . . . Oh-h-h." From the river, a noise Tony would remember for the rest of his life. The sad, melancholy cry surrounded him, stirred up an emotion he couldn't understand, and Tony's eyes filled with tears. The crying came from a woman who wanted something so bad it was killing her not to have it.

Johnny found him at the river's edge, softly crying that he wanted to help her. Johnny said it was La Llorona, and it was time to go home. As they walked away, Tony looked back at the river and saw a woman dressed in black, wandering along the bank.

That night Adolfo listened, nodded his head and declared, "La Llorona, *hijo*. The woman condemned by God to roam the earth searching for her children, children she threw away years ago."

Adolfo held his glass of liquor in small, bony hands. The veins in his arms popped out on his skin. Their gray color deepened to blue as he drank more Jim Beam. His hair was thin and white, his moustache full and gray. Gold glistened from the corner of a smile that stretched from his black, moist eyes to the wrinkled, grizzled chin.

Jesusita hollered from the kitchen where she stirred a pot of beans. "*¡Viejo! ¡Déjalo!* These things are not for children. *Mira, no más*. You will make him afraid to go to sleep, afraid of his own shadow. *Quítate con tus mentiras*." Her words were wasted on the old man and boy who were determined that the story be told.

"She was a young woman, beautiful, of course, with a dark, Indian face framed by long, rich, black hair. Every man wanted her, but she wanted only one—Don Antonio, rancher, richest man in the valley. And he fell for her, hard. They were more in love than two people have a right to expect in this world. They prospered in wealth, influence and happiness. They had three children, one after another, two boys and a girl who mirrored her beautiful mother."

Tony had no problem imagining the mother and children.

"That was where the love story went bad, *niño*. Don Antonio loved the children with a generosity that bordered on the hysterical. He showered the babies with gifts they couldn't use for years—fancy mechanical toys, horses, clothes, even money piled up in their rooms. He watched over them with a single-mindedness that caused him to neglect his ranch. He gave them so much love that he had little left for his wife. Oh, he loved her, that was still true. But the feeling he had for the children was overwhelming, all powerful. And the woman could feel the difference."

Tony marveled at the love a parent could show for his children.

"Soon the woman blamed the children for the lack of fire in her husband's lovemaking. She saw them as rivals. She remembered the early days of her romance with the Don, the greatest love she had ever known, and she hated the children for taking it away. She had to do something, she was desperate, on the edge of losing everything she had ever wanted. She turned to the devil and his ways for help."

Adolfo stopped and slowly sipped his drink. He stared into the dark liquid and rolled it in the glass. Tony waited, nervously anticipating the story.

"*Pues, tú sabes, 'jito.* In those days it was much easier to deal with the devil than it is now. *Brujas* were everywhere. A person only had to ask the right one to get what he wanted. My own mother asked one for help for my father because of the illness he suffered for months that made him weak, unable to work or do much else. The witch gave my mother a smelly salve she rubbed on my father and it worked. It only cost my mother a few hours of work *por la bruja.*"

The old man whispered the word *bruja* each time he said it, making it sound sinister and threatening.

"The woman sought the help of one of the bad *brujas.* Their plan was to take the children to the river, where the devil would trade Don Antonio's love for the little ones. On the night of the exchange, driven by jealousy, she threw them into the rushing water."

Tony gulped down the last of his drink and tried not to think of drowning babies.

"Then, son, she learned the lesson all who deal with the devil must learn sooner or later. He doesn't keep his part of the bargain. Don Antonio never loved her again, *con razón. Se murió de sentimiento por sus niños.* His last words were that he hated her and he would see her again in hell. She wasn't that lucky. She tried to undo her evil but that was impossible. The *bruja* disappeared, and no other would talk to her, much less give her any help. Priests avoided her. Church doors were slammed in her face. *La mujer se volvió loca.*"

Tony heard the words as if they came from God.

"She convinced herself that the children were alive. She said they floated down the river and were waiting for her to find them and take them home. She followed rivers to their end, crying for her children, but she never found them. To this day she wanders the earth looking for the children, crying for them. And to this day she is despised and hated for what she did."

But Tony didn't hate her; he thought he understood. She was a mother looking for her lost children, a woman like his own mother who regretted giving him away and now wanted him back. She was sorry and he realized he needed to go to her.

The sounds at the river were heard by others, and soon the small town was caught up in the myth of La Llorona. People parked their cars along the highway and sat on fenders and bumpers, cameras and binoculars pointed at the river. Women fingered rosaries and men had handguns hanging from their belts.

The older boys treated the story of La Llorona as a joke. They made ugly faces at the younger children and told crude stories about an old woman under the bridge. Johnny coerced his friends into searching for the source of the moaning. He wanted to show everyone that La Llorona was just another fairy story, another fantasy of old Mexicans.

Tony knew the truth. He spent hours planning how to bring his mother back to him, how to find her and lead her away from the maze she was trapped in by the river. Jesusita saw that he was deep in concentration and she warned, "The boy who spends too much time thinking is the one who ends up with more problems. Get out and play, *'jito*, outside, *con tus hermanos y no pienses tanto.*"

The night of the search, Johnny wore his best pair of khakis. His hair was brushed back in a ducktail. A gold crucifix hung from his neck. He put a card with a picture of the Virgin Mary in his wallet. He told Jesusita he was going to a movie and then spend the night at a friend's. She didn't believe him but she knew at seventeen he was almost a man and could not be told what to do by an old lady. She patted his arm and advised him, "*Con cuidao.*"

Tony decided he had to keep Johnny away from the crying woman. After Johnny left, Tony paced nervously, shouting and slapping at the younger children, driving them to tears with his craziness. When the house was finally quiet, all the kids and *abuelitos* in bed, he sneaked out the back door. He grabbed a bicycle and rode through the dark town to the river.

The day's heat lingered. The night had a heavy, stuffy feeling. The air was clean and still. Tony rode under long, gray shadows cast by trees in the moonlight.

Details stood out. He saw numbers on houses, hopscotch patterns on the sidewalks. Fireflies flitted around the hedge near the library, where he turned onto the street that led to the river. A few bats circled the trees but he ignored them.

He concentrated on the face of his mother. She was sorry, loving, eager for him.

Tony parked the bicycle at the edge of the woods and walked into the darkness of the trees. He avoided thick clumps of bushes and weeds.

Bright stars hung over the hills beyond the edge of the highway. A dog or coyote howled in the darkness. Owls hooted sadly.

He stared at the river, the moon, the trees. No one appeared to talk to him, to take him home. He threw flat rocks at the river, immediately frustrated with his bad luck. He walked towards the bicycle.

"Oh-h-h. Oh-h-h." The suddenness of the crying made him jump. It started low and soft, slowly increasing with intensity.

The wind stirred the trees and shadows danced on the ground. Tony felt the earth move.

The moaning was loud, vibrant.

He thought he saw shooting stars fall behind the trees. A cloud covered the moon and Tony was in darkness.

He heard footsteps behind him. He turned but there was nothing. He heard other sounds from other directions. Things seemed to move in the bushes.

The moaning covered the sound of the river. The wind whipped dust in small whirlpools around Tony.

Tony knew he had made a mistake. He did not belong near the river looking for a woman who drowned children. He tried to calm himself with thoughts of his lost mother but they were not the good ones he needed. He wanted to be home with his grandmother, with the flesh and blood person who loved him and cared for him better than any imaginary mother. He wanted to run but he forgot where he left his bicycle. Sobs came out of his throat in hiccups.

Then he saw her.

The woman in black walked to him with open arms. She was beautiful. Coal black eyes pierced into his, asking him to come to her. "*Hijo . . . niño. Vente conmigo, tu mamá. Niño-ohh . . . niño-ohh.*" Her voice reminded him of the train whistle he heard rushing by every night.

Dark red lips formed a kiss she blew to Tony. "*Niño . . . corazón, niño-ohh.*" Her hands beckoned him. Tony stepped towards her, driven by his need to know.

"Run, Tony, run!" Johnny hollered from a hundred yards away. Tony saw him running, holding a long stick in his hands. He started to tell Johnny it was no sweat, man, this was his mother, his old lady.

A loud hiss stopped him. His beautiful mother changed into an ugly, grotesque creature. Lumps and oozing pustules covered her skin. Ragged teeth grinned evilly at him. Patches of scalp gleamed beneath strands of wispy hair. The eyes were red-orange balls.

She lunged at him.

"Run, Tony, run. Get the hell out of there!"

Fingernails scraped his back. He dodged her by twisting as he ran to Johnny. "Move, you little shit. Run! Run!"

It grabbed Tony. He felt a warm, slimy arm wrap around his waist. He smelled the sweet, putrid odor he remembered from the time he found a dead chicken in the coop.

He screamed.

He kicked at the thing that had him. He saw a light flash, felt a thud on his back. He fell to the ground and though he tried to stop, he threw up. He sobbed into the earth until Johnny picked him up and carried him to the car.

Years later, as Tony again lay crying in the dirt, in a place he had not known existed, Adolfo told Tony he knew what had happened, and he was sorry he couldn't have helped the boy back when he was sick with fear and loneliness. "But *hijo*, now you can rest. You can come home with me."

KITE LESSON

Florence, Colorado, 1955

Luis was seven when his father bought a kite and tried to teach him how to fly it. They walked from their house to the baseball field, overgrown with weeds, and waited for the wind to gather.

Luis stood in silence, away from the action.

Emilio was all business as he put together the plastic blue and red thing, attached the string and added a tail of old rags. When he finished his preparations the man chased away the dogs that sniffed at the contraption. He watched the sky for a hint of turbulence, a sign that it was time to launch the toy.

"I learned how to fly kites from my brother Danny. He knew so much about everything, son, so much. He was only nineteen when they killed him in Korea. He would've been a great man. Strong, smart. He taught me about life when I was no older than you, Luis. Lessons that a man needs to know to survive. *La vida es dura.*"

Luis nodded but, as usual, his father lost him. He had heard the story of Danny many times. Emilio's eyes filled with sadness as he spoke of his dead brother. The boy was puzzled by the man's insistence on remembering.

The wind rose to a level that appeared to be right. Luis grabbed the kite and held it aloft, causing the wind to catch it. His father clutched the string.

"You should master this art, boy. And it is an art, after all, as well as a science. Kites show the delicate balance between security and the animal urge to let go, to live life in the clouds. *¿Entiendes, chico?*"

He jerked the string and the kite jumped.

"Let it go, Luis, let the damn thing go." He led the kite into the sky.

It was a beautiful kite. It lazily drifted upward to the full white clouds. Sunlight flashed off the plastic sheen creating red, blue and gold streaks.

Emilio reeled out yard after yard of string. The kite hungrily accepted the freedom. The man laughed and hollered and jumped among the weeds.

"There it goes, boy, there it goes! Our kite is now flying with the birds and we did it, we broke the law of gravity. My brother was right."

The boy watched the floating, tiny speck of color. He saw birds near the kite, the tail flapping crazily; and he heard his father's laugh, but Luis couldn't understand.

"*Hijo*, take the string, fly this baby."

Emilio offered the ball of string. He laid it in the boy's hand.

"Let it drift with the breeze. No need to give it any more slack, it's plenty high already."

Luis never held the ball. He felt it slip from his hand, saw it drag along the ground. Slowly it rose, so slowly that for years when he thought of this day it was in slow motion black and white. He ran after the string but it was above his head. Suddenly it took off with more speed than the boy had experienced in all of his short life.

Emilio jumped for the string but it was gone. He turned, looked at Luis, then shook his head. He kicked at the dirt with his boot, shrugged weary shoulders and walked back to the house.

The kite disappeared over the trees. Luis stared at the empty sky. When he looked for his father, the man was blocks away. Luis ran but he couldn't catch up to him.

SENTIMENTAL VALUE

1988

The Sunday insert, tucked in among the comics and grocery coupons, had a three-page, color, baseball article. *Latin American Ball Players. Latin Stars of the National Pastime. The Latin American Connection.* Latin?

Plenty of hype about the current crop of players. Sure, they were good. Who wouldn't want Canseco, or Valenzuela? And some of them born in the States. But they couldn't be bat boys for Cepeda, Aparicio, Marichal or Zorro—Zoilo Versalles, MVP that year it all changed for Ray. He had read about these players when he was growing up, had kept their cardboard images in a box with his glove. They were the men who inspired the skinny, quiet Raymond López.

He had been fast. Fifty stolen bases his senior year, good hands, a better bat. Ah, but his arm. *¡A toda madre!* A cannon that made him famous, a starter for four years at North High and a City League All Star right fielder. That arm generated a couple of calls from bald, short guys in plaid sport coats who said they were scouts. Talk about characters! Smoking their smelly cigars, going on about the big leagues like Ray was the next bonus baby and it was right around the corner.

"Just sign this contract and we'll hook you up in the Instructional League, buy your momma a house one of these days, boy. A little extra in it *(and for you, too, Mr. Scout, as long as you got my name on a piece of paper that locks me in forever, but if, just if, mind you, if I don't cut it, phfft! So long, boy!)* We'll even cover your bus ticket to spring training."

Mamá wanted Ray to continue with school, a community college, and that was fine with the scouts, but they couldn't provide any help.

"Let's see how you do against stiffer competition, boy, then we can talk about financial assistance."

And then the scouts shook their heads, flicked the ashes off their cigars and walked away, muttering about the waste of time, late for the next Latin or Black or farm kid with the strong arm, fast legs, quick bat.

Clemente. Had to be included. Roberto Clemente. Nice picture, good looking guy, for a P.R. First Latin in the Hall of Fame. Exactly 3000 hits. Lifetime .317. Played in fourteen World Series games and hit in every one. The long throw to Sanguillén at home, right on the money, and you're out! Yeah, yeah, everyone knew about the New Year's Eve mercy mission, the horrible plane crash and the special election to the Hall of Fame. So what? Ray knew what was really important about Clemente.

No mention, this time, of how they all hated him. Even Ray understood that and he was just a kid during that 1960 season when the writers bypassed "Bob" for MVP and gave it to Groat. Clemente had to wait six years, and by then Ray had forgotten about a baseball career.

The usual quote not included.

"The Latin player doesn't get the recognition he deserves. Neither does the Negro unless he does something really spectacular."

Not that kind of feature.

Ray trimmed the pages of the article, carefully applied glue to the edges and gently centered them in a scrapbook. He waited for the glue to dry, took one last look at Clemente, then returned the scrapbook to the makeshift shelf where it sat with a dozen other scrapbooks. He threw the rest of the paper in the trash. It was time for Christina, and he had to get ready. He pushed himself into the bathroom and began the ordeal of cleaning his body.

The hot towel felt good on his arms and chest. Of course, he couldn't feel it on his legs, what was left of them. Only three weeks since her last visit and he was horny as a teenaged kid. Business had been good, thank God. Pumping his sax for the tourists down in LoDo might not sound like a real gig but he made enough to pay the rent on his dump, eat a couple times a day and every once in a while buy a bottle of Old Crow, or something close.

He anticipated her touch, her mouth, the feel of her breasts in his hands, the sounds she made when he worked his Chicano magic on her. God, he was hot already. Think of something else, man, don't get too worked up, or Christina won't have anything to do.

Lefty Gómez, half-Spanish, half-Irish. Ray couldn't believe it when he read about Lefty in the *Baseball Almanac*. He assumed that the great Yankee pitcher, winner of the first All Star Game, was a Chicano from California (he wouldn't have been *Chicano*, of course—what would they have called him back then?), but there it was, half-Spanish, half-Irish. A cover? Apparently not. "El Gómez," "Goofy." Colorful nicknames for a colorful personality, everyone said. One of the greatest, but Ray still felt disappointment because Lefty wasn't *raza*.

Ray had a way with baseball. He knew from the day he picked up a bat and hit his father's first toss back at the old man and knocked him on his butt. Ray Sr., shouted, "Wise ass," and threw him some smoke. Ray swung and missed, but he stood his ground and the old man got this gleam in his eyes and a smile about a mile wide. Then he tried a curve, and damn if little Ray didn't drill it in the direction of first base. Ray Sr., couldn't spend a lot of time with little Ray, working at night, on the weekends, or on the road, doing anything to hustle a buck, but when he had a few hours they gathered the mitts and balls and bats he had scrounged from second-hand stores and junk dealers, and father and son played ball.

Ray slipped on his cleanest shirt. Christina liked him to be fresh and neat, she demanded it, and at fifty bucks a shot he thought he should try to maintain some standards. She was his last luxury, his only extravagance.

Why would the old man, a wetback orphan with a wife and three of his own kids before he was twenty years old, on the edge of big city desperation, pick up on American baseball? It could be something as simple as playing the game in an overgrown field somewhere on the outskirts of Durango, Mexico. Sneaking in to watch winter ball. Sal Maglie and those other *gabacho* players who told the major leagues to get screwed, for a couple of years anyway, and then crossed the border to keep in shape, make their fortunes, until they realized where their bread really was buttered. Or it could be—he never let on—that the old man understood the more complex things in life, like the fact that his kids were definitely not Mexicans, and although they carried tags like Chicano or *cholo* or pachuco, they were American, even if he wasn't, just not quite as American as the snot-nosed, blond-haired children who wanted to play with little Ray, and what could be more American than baseball?

Nah. The old man just liked to play ball.

He rushed to the door when he heard the knock. Christina waited for him, smiling.

"Ray, how've you been? We got to get together more often, baby. I kind of missed you."

Christina earned her money. She bent over and planted a kiss on Ray's lips that almost raised him out of the chair, a crane lifting steel girders. She tongued him, rubbed his back, brought him back to life—miracle worker Christina!—then eased up.

"How about a drink, Ray? I got some time."

Ray poured the last two shots from his bottle, then pulled two beers from the fridge and twisted off the tops with an easy flick. His meaty arms and thick wrists looked as if they could swing a forty ounce bat with the precision of Ernie Banks.

"How's your boy, Christina? Haven't seen little Julián for months. Must be big, eh?"

"Jules, Ray. His name's Jules. He ain't no Spanish kid. He's a terror. Can't keep up with him. He's got all this energy, the terrible twos."

She swallowed the shot in one gulp and sipped the beer.

Ray could see the tiredness around her eyes, but he didn't check her out too closely. She was sensitive about her looks. Ray thought she was fine. She liked to show her legs. She wore tight skirts with slits up the side, or skirts so short that Ray knew before they had a date that she had a rose tattooed on her thigh. Ray told her, often, that she would be surprised how good she would look and feel if she laid off the coke. She needed it, she would answer with a grunt. Her line of work required something to get over, something to take off the edge.

In any event, she was getting old, she said, especially for what she did, and the extra dose of "fire in the blood" kept her on her feet, and her back.

But, damn, Ray was already in his forties, what the hell can you do about getting old? Did Ray Sr., get old, was he even alive, did he ever think about playing catch with little Ray?

"Bring him by, Christina. I'll show him my scrapbooks, teach him how to play ball."

"Oh, Ray. He's too little. He'll tear up your books. Maybe when he's older. You guys can play catch or something. Or teach him how to play some music."

Sure, Christina, whatever.

She stretched a line of powder on his wobbly table and snorted it quicker than Ray could get it together to object.

"*Oh yeah,*" she whispered.

Her eyes glazed and a faint reddish tint crept up her jaw line. She breathed deeply for a few minutes, then she shook her head and gave Ray one of the smiles that filled his dreams. She walked around the room, stepping out of pieces of clothing, and Ray watched in silence. He loved it when she stripped for him. Lacy black things with hooks and straps hung on her skin, jiggling when she moved slowly towards him. The rose sat like a bruise on her leg, warm and swollen, ready for his caress. She stood at the edge of his desk, turned away from him so that he could watch her wiggle her ass.

"Ray, you never showed me this. Wha's it?"

She held a baseball in her hands.

"Uh, Christina, be careful. My old man got me that. Here, give it to me."

And although he didn't want to ruin the mood, he rolled to her with a little too much speed, a little too much urgency in his response, and snatched the ball from her hand.

"I's jus' a ball, ain't it?" Her words slipped out half-formed. She wasn't wiggling anymore.

Ray relented. He handed it back to Christina.

"All right. But be careful. See, there it is, Roberto Clemente's autograph. The old man got it for me one time when he worked in L.A. Clemente signed it before a game with the Dodgers. He's dead, you know."

"Your old man?"

"Clemente. Plane crash. The ball's worth a lot of money. But it's about the only thing I got from my old man, so it's kind of special to me."

Christina returned the ball to its space on Ray's desk.

"You kept it all these years? How old's it?"

"Early sixties. I was a kid. Actually, I lost it, didn't know what the hell happened to it. But when my mother died, I came back from Nam for the funeral, and there it was in a box with her rosaries, pictures and mantillas. She didn't have much. For some reason she kept this old ball."

Christina watched him drift away. His scarred face saddened, his body slumped in the wheelchair. She took his head in her hands and held him against her, smoothed the strands of wispy hair and helped Ray in the only way she knew.

* * *

Clyde tried to stay calm. But handling his habit was not an experience that lent itself to calmness. And making the money by breaking into houses, apartments and an occasional second-hand store, the kind that should not have alarms, only added to the tension. No wonder he always felt tired—except when he was riding the blow, of course. Then he could do anything, anytime, anywhere. Make love to the most beautiful woman. Pull off the most outrageous heist in thief history. Kick ass. Be the man.

Ripping off old Ray's sax didn't exactly fall into the historical category. Stealing the cripple's instrument, Ray's source of income, probably ranked as outrageous—pitiful but outrageous.

He tried to explain to Linda but she didn't get it.

"I can get twenty, thirty bucks for the sax. Ray keeps it in good shape. Take me five minutes to get it, maybe. His lock's gotta be a joke. And what can Ray do about it if I get in his crib and yank the sax? Not a damn thing. Nothin'."

Linda arched her eyebrows.

"But, crap, Clyde. It's Ray. He don't harm no one. He's a little weird, but who around here ain't? And you know him, man. He knows you, too. What if he sees you? What if he turns you into the cops? You ready for that?"

Clyde knew there was one thing he definitely was not ready for, and that was another lock-up. He refused to consider the possibility.

"No way there's any risk. Ray drinks himself to sleep every night. Calls the juice his Oblivion Express. I heard him talkin' about it one day when he was on the corner playing for handouts, explainin' to that Jesus Saves preacher why he can't get up early for the coffee and donuts and sermon at the center. Goes out like a match in the wind. And in his chair, you think he's goin' to pull any hero stuff? Come on, it's a setup. Made for Clyde the Glide, smoothest second-story pro on the West Side."

Linda shook her head but she knew it was hopeless. And maybe Clyde could scrape enough together for a line or two, if he did an all-nighter and hit at least a half-dozen places. Ray's sax by itself wouldn't pay for a taste, much less a good time. It was stupid but it was Clyde's lifestyle, so to speak. To each his own.

***

Ray slept curled in a ball in his chair, clutching the saxophone he dreamed was his rifle. The street below his room shook with the noise from buses and taxis, ambulances screaming their warnings to the dealers, pimps and winos prowling Ray's neighborhood. He slept through it all. He prowled, too, but the thick jungle that surrounded him held more terror than the actors in the midnight street scene could conjure in their wildest, drug-induced fantasies. He moaned and twisted his blanket into a sweaty, crumpled rag, but he slept.

The door creaked—damn cheap lock—and Ray's eyes jerked open. For a horrible, ridiculous second, slant-eyed killers hovered around him, poked at him with their weapons, and Ray whimpered. The door eased shut and a shadow moved around the room. Street lights bounced off the gleam of a knife blade.

"Get the hell out of here!"

Before the guy could react, Ray wheeled into the back of the intruder, rammed and knocked him over.

"What the . . . !"

The knife flew across the room. Clyde crawled across the floor, looking for the weapon, trying to regain the advantage. Ray ran over groping hands. A feeble scream mixed with the loud crunch of fractured bone. The thief struggled to his feet, turned around in circles, lost in the darkness, defenseless against the crip he thought would be easy. Ray moved smoothly, effortlessly. His strong, solid fingers grabbed the first thing they touched and flung it at the man. Dazed, Clyde stumbled out the door and collapsed at the bottom of the stairs.

Ray's neighbors flicked on their lights, threw open their doors, some with guns in their hands, and kicked the intruder sniveling on the stained, muddy carpet.

Ray wheeled to the hallway and picked up his baseball. The ink had been smeared by the impact on the burglar's greasy skin.

***

He held the ball with his vise-like grip and carefully, slowly, used a Sharpie to fill in the words *Roberto Clemente* over the smudge.

Someone nudged his shoulder.

"Better get that door fixed, Ray. I walked right in. You okay?"

"Yeah, Art. Guess I still got my throwing arm. I think I know that guy. You recognize him?"

"No way. Dirty creeps around here. About time one of them got it. You really clobbered him. What the hell you hit him with?"

"This ball. Check it out. My old man gave it to me, about the only thing I got from him. It's worth some money, but it means more to me, it's kind of special. Sentimental value and all that."

2012

The taquitos are crunchy, tasty, better when dipped in the *queso fundido* sauce. You try to eat while you read Bolaño's story in *The New Yorker*. You know you won't finish the piece. You haven't finished anything by him since *Distant Star* (you loved it). Did not start *2666*.

The noisy restaurant is crowded, like so many places at the beginning of the new year. Is it approved to call this business, with its uniformed help, fast-food counter, mass-produced dishes and serve-yourself-salsa table, a restaurant? You easily could develop minor hysteria over the commotion and chaos but you feel at ease because the entire staff, visible to every customer as they frantically prepare burritos, salads and chicken bowls, is Latino. That is to say, dark, foreign and accented, like you.

The cooks prepare several dishes at once, then slide them onto a gleaming metal shelf. A man, slightly older than the others but still young, takes the completed orders and barks out numbers. "Ninety-five. Ninety-six. Eighty-nine." Customers look at their receipts. The lucky ones get their orders quickly. Those who asked for extra cheese or a substitution of pinto for black beans, wait longer. These often ask the number barker if he missed their number. He always says no.

You are not the only dark-skinned patron but you are outnumbered by the mostly youthful, mostly white lunchtime customers who have escaped their employment for a quick meal. Why do you persist in thinking in racial terms? You have been hobbled for as long as you can remember by covert restraints, imposed by outside antagonists or adopted by you in defense. What is worse—the hobbles or the waste of time contemplating their origins?

You give up on the story and turn your attention to the girl waiting at the counter in the teal leotards and feathered hat. Her ass is appealing. She rubs the palm of her left hand across her right shoulder. A thoughtless gesture, by which you mean she did not think about it before she made it, not that she is careless. The provocative movement causes the man behind her to smirk as though he knows what she intended. You are aware that every man in the restaurant watches her. A few women nod. They are in on the secret, whatever that may be. The girl moves from the counter to wait for her order. Her lipstick is striking. Perhaps you are intrigued by her lips, which are fleshy and recall plums or a peeled orange. You drop your eyes when she looks in your direction. You remind yourself that she is very young and then you are struck by how obnoxious that would sound if you uttered it aloud. You focus on your food.

You close the magazine but not before you jump pages and read the last words of Bolaño's story. "He has an erection and yet he doesn't feel sexually aroused in any way." You cannot ignore the conclusion that you are aroused and yet you do not have an erection, in any way.

FENCE BUSTERS

"who journeyed to Denver, who died in Denver, who came back to Denver & waited in vain, who watched over Denver & brooded & loned in Denver and finally went away to find out the Time, & now Denver is lonesome for her heroes"
Allen Ginsberg, *Howl*

Kiko tugged on the short brim of his cap, a *cachucha* to his mother, and adjusted the strap of his shoeshine box. Thick black hair clumped around the edges of the cap. An October gust streaked up Larimer Street. He squinted to block dust stirred from the curb.

Kiko heard the announcer before he saw the radio. He felt the speaker's excitement but the boy didn't care much about the game. The Dodgers weren't in it, again.

"Covington's sac fly to Mantle scores Mathews and ties the score at three in the eighth inning. These pesky Milwaukee Braves won't give up."

He slipped the card out of his shirt pocket and looked at it for the hundredth time that day. *Rival Fence Busters.* Willie Mays wore a magnificent smile as he admired Duke Snider's muscular right arm. His father said it wasn't much of a tip. Kiko disagreed. It might have been his best tip ever.

Kiko nodded at the man sprawled in the entrance to El Charrito. A torn and stained overcoat partially covered the wino's dusty pants and shirt. Kiko's mother called the bums *desgraciados*, but his father said that word was mighty fancy for men who lived on skid row.

Hank won't be there long, Kiko thought. He peered into the café and breathed the familiar smells of roasted chile, fried beans and warm tortillas, but it was a mistake to allow the smells to linger. He had at least three hours before he returned home, and supper.

"Hey, Shiner," Hank murmured. "Spare a dime? I could use a cup a coffee."

"*No hablo inglés*," Kiko lied.

"Come on. You know me. I helped your old man move all that junk into your house. Don't give me that no in-gless stuff. You speak English good as me. For a Mex."

"I need lunch money. Why do you think I'm out here on Wednesday? You better move. Here comes Wanda."

The waitress gripped a broom as she marched to the doorway. The men listening to the game cheered her on.

"Get 'em, Wanda! *¡Ándale!* Throw 'em out!"

"Avay from 'yer! Ya' stinkin' up da place!" Her jowls jiggled and sweat dotted the white skin above her bright red lips.

Kiko smiled. Her words sounded funnier than a regular *gabacha*, another word from his mother. When Kiko mentioned her, his sister Elena said that the waitress was Polish and Kiko had to ask his teacher what that meant.

He tipped his cap, as his father had taught him. Wanda winked. She slammed the broom across Hank's legs and a cloud of dried mud and stale wine exploded.

Kiko headed for the new restaurant, just opened by the Silvas fresh from Chihuahua. The place might have men who needed clean shoes for the weekend, who had twenty-five cents for the brightest shine in Denver and who wouldn't joke about Mexicans.

He waited for traffic to thin out and then crossed Twenty-first, in the direction of the downtown skyscrapers and construction projects. Mariachi music seeped through the walls of the American Inn. Kiko recognized the tune, something his mother listened to. He thought about going inside, but reconsidered. Too early for dance hall men.

He sauntered past the glass panes of Johnnie's Market and avoided the wide-eyed stare of the hairless goat head perched next to jars of pickled pigs' feet, bags of *hojas* for tamales, *ristras* of dark chiles, sacks of beans.

Kiko stopped at the Monterey House. He smelled fresh paint. A sign in the window said *Open*, but something was wrong. A few adults and several children gathered in the middle of the large room, but there was no food and no one looked like a customer.

He inched into the doorway. The oldest man shook his head as he rocked on his boot heels and his chair's back legs. "No lights," he said. "Maybe next week." The man turned to a woman standing behind him. "I didn't know about no deposit for Public Service. How was I to know?" he asked in Spanish.

Kiko trekked on. He hadn't made any money all afternoon. His father often teased him about the lack of income from his shoe-shining job. "You spend hours *en las calles*, and you come back with maybe *cincuenta centavos*? Less than a dollar? *¿Cómo*? How does that happen? There are hundreds of men in this city who need clean shoes. Businessmen, bankers, *abogados*. All you got to do is ask, *m'ijo*. Just ask. That's how it is in this country. Do something for them, and they have the money to pay. *A eso le dicen la oportunidad*."

Opportunity. Kiko had his doubts. He switched the strap again and rubbed his shoulder. His mother would want to massage him with *osha*. His arms were tired, his feet hot and grimy and his cap too tight. He walked for several minutes without realizing where he was going. He ambled to a stop, like a car out of gas. The sign over his head announced Cantina. Bar. Café. El Chapultepec. He walked in.

Baseball played in the background.

"What a finish. Adcock scores on Bruton's single in the tenth and the Braves win Game One of the 1958 World Series. Another outstanding performance by Spahn—he went the distance."

Stools rested against the bar and booths hugged the wall. Kiko only glanced at the large mirror behind the bar but he had an impression of decorated boats, flowers floating on water and men in large straw hats.

Two men sat in a booth, drinking beer and smoking cigarettes. They stared at the boy. Kiko thought he saw one of the men spit on the floor under their table. Another man leaned on the bar, half-on and half-off a stool.

"The Braves? Give me a break," the man on the stool said.

The bartender poured whisky into the man's glass. "Where's your Red Sox, Jack? When's the last time they were in the Series?"

Jack groaned.

Kiko took a deep breath.

"Shoe shine? Only a quarter for the best shine in Denver."

Jack looked down at Kiko. The bartender said, "Leave my customers alone . . . " but Jack raised his hand and the bartender shrugged. Jack wore a blue wrinkled shirt, a cap that looked like Kiko's, except more ragged, and cracked brown loafers. Not the signs of a man who cared about the luster of his shoes. Kiko turned to leave.

"Why not?"

"You sure, Jack?" the bartender asked.

"Yeah, Jimmy. It's all right. The last time I got a shine was in Denver. Seems like a karmic thing to do." He sat down on the edge of a booth.

Kiko knelt on the floor and opened his box, exposing rags, brushes and a foot rest carved by his father. He took out a tin of shoe wax. Jack lifted his right shoe to the foot rest.

Kiko concentrated on his work. "What's your name, kid?" Jack asked.

"Francisco, but everyone calls me Kiko. Some are calling me Shiner."

"Shiner? I like that. It could mean different things. Words are like that. Different meanings depending on the talker, so in the end they don't mean anything at all."

Jack took off his cap and his hair lay smashed against his forehead. His eyes were ringed with dark, puffy skin.

"If you say so, mister."

"Yeah. If I say so. You from here, Shiner?"

"Curtis Street. Over a few blocks."

"I know where Curtis is. We watched baseball near there, on Welton. Years ago. Good crowds back then. Those kids were serious about their ball playing. Whites and Negroes; Mexicans, Indians. All kinds. In team uniforms. That was cool."

Kiko wasn't sure if he should respond. "I guess," he said.

"I used to live here. My best friend is from here. We had good and bad times in this town, but they were all good when you think of it." He paused. "What I meant was, you born here? In the States?"

Kiko flinched. He had heard this kind of talk before. His parents spoke to him about being a citizen of the United States, no matter what anyone said. He had every *pinche* right to be here. That's how his father put it.

"Yeah."

"That's good. Something to be proud of. Born into the mystery of this country, and the dream. Just don't let them get you down."

Kiko's customers said many strange things while he popped his rags over their shoes. His father told him to ignore the strangeness: "I don't understand these people. That's up to you to figure out, *m'ijo*. Until then, do the job and get paid."

Kiko bent closer to the shoe to rub extra hard on the thin leather. The baseball card slid out of his pocket.

"What's that?" Jack asked.

Kiko picked up the card by the tip of a corner and handed it to Jack. He hoped he hadn't smudged it.

"This is great. I saw these two play when they were in New York."

"You did? In person? Playing baseball?"

Jack laughed. "Sure, kid. I watched Mays and Snider go head-to-head, a couple of times. Mays was like an antelope in the outfield, maybe a jaguar, but I never saw a jaguar, so I can't say for sure. And Snider? Flatbush royalty. But I was at Yankee Stadium when the Red Sox were in town."

Kiko finished the shoe. He stretched. Jack returned the card.

"You ever talk with them?" Kiko asked.

"Shiner, you wouldn't believe. I've been at parties with guys like this. I signed a book for the Duke. And he autographed a ball for me."

"The kid don't know what you're talkin' about," Jimmy said. "Jack's a writer. Kind of famous these days because of his book from last year. There's no livin' with him now. I remember when he was just another barfly, him and his crazy pals. Bunch of goofs and drunks and so-called poets. Jack put them in his stories and now he's the toast of the upper crust. Goes to show."

"Come on, Jimmy. Don't you give me a hard time, too."

Jimmy turned off the small television set. He walked around the bar to the jukebox. He pressed a switch and the box came to life with running streams of light and a soft hum. A tube of blue light surrounded the gold and red machine like a halo. Jimmy punched a few buttons and music played.

"Blakey and Monk," Jack mumbled. "Johnnie Griffin. Nice." His head bounced to saxophone and piano riffs.

Kiko decided he liked the music. He was almost done with Jack's shoes.

"Whatever happened to that friend of yours?" Jimmy asked. "That car-thievin' wild kid? I ain't seen him for years."

Jack lit a cigarette. "Let me get my drink, Shiner." He stood up, walked over to the bar and lifted his glass. He finished what was left of the whisky and coughed.

"Neal's in California."

"That right?" Jimmy responded. "What's he gonna do there he can't do here? Too many people on the Coast already. Denver's just right for me."

"He wants to leave. Always on the move, running from something. But he's stuck now."

"Why's that?"

"He checked into the Hotel San Quentin. Got a lease for something like ten years."

"Who'd he kill? The Pope?"

"Just tried to be free in the land of the free but now he knows that freedom is a crime, and it's sure not free. Or something like that." His words cracked with a half-laugh, half-sigh. He sat back down.

"He should'a never left Denver," Jimmy said.

"We all leave some day. Neal can't stop leaving. I worry that he's anchored for years. It could kill him." He inhaled smoke and then tapped his cigarette in an ashtray that looked like a Mexican sombrero. "I made the book people pay for a trip to Denver. They got me everywhere else selling books that haven't been written. I thought I owed it to Neal, but now I don't know why I'm here. It's not the same."

Kiko replaced the cap on the tin and tossed it into the box. He folded his buffing rag, placed it in the box, wiped his hands on another rag and shut his box.

Jack admired his shoes. The cracks were still visible and the worn heels would never be replaced but the leather gleamed like clean rain on a new highway.

"That should impress the Hollywood wolves waiting to tear me apart." He pulled a crunched dollar bill from his pants pocket. "Keep the change."

Kiko touched his cap with his fingertips. "Thanks, mister. Much appreciated."

"Send that greaser over here. I could use a shine, but I ain't payin' no buck. Maybe a dime, if he's any good." One of the men sitting at the booth pointed at his shoes. His drinking partner grunted a laugh.

"Sorry, mister. It's a quarter for a shine," Kiko said.

"Just get your brown ass over here."

"It's a quarter, mister."

"Shine my shoes and you'll get what you get, which might be a whippin' if I don't like the job you do."

The friend grunted again. A toothy grin creased his face and his eyes lit up in expectation. "You tell him, Leonard."

"Hey, knock it off," Jimmy said. "No call for that."

"Mind your business. I don't like dirty Mexicans hanging around when I drink my beer. And I really don't like the ones who talk back." Leonard chugged his drink. "I had my doubts about this place, just from the spic name. I told you that, didn't I, Tom?" Tom nodded eagerly. "You don't run a respectable joint," Leonard continued. "You let in those kind."

"Get out!" Jimmy shouted.

The two men stood up. Leonard grabbed Kiko's shoulder and squeezed. The boy tripped over his box and fell. His cap rolled down his back.

Jack jumped to his feet. "You're tough with a kid. Try someone your own size."

Leonard threw a punch that missed. Jack grabbed Leonard's shirt collar with his left hand and swung his right fist into Leonard's jaw. Kiko heard a loud crack. Leonard dropped to his knees. Tom moved to jump on Jack but Jimmy had rushed from behind the bar. He held a baseball bat.

"Scram! Take this piece of crap with you," Jimmy said.

Tom picked up Leonard by the armpits and pushed him through the door. Leonard cupped his jaw. Tom hollered ugly curses, but the two men did not look back.

A man in a suit walked in. "What's going on here? That man looked hurt. Another fight? You drunk again?"

Jack's laugh drowned the jukebox. "Not yet, Perry. But very soon, that's a promise."

Perry grabbed Jack by the elbow and started to guide him out. "We're almost late for the college. I can't leave you for a half-hour without some disaster happening. Come on, let's go."

Jack twisted free. He stacked dollar bills on the bar. "Thanks, Jimmy. Next time."

Jimmy shook Jack's hand. "Anytime."

"Take care of yourself, Shiner. Like I said, don't let the sons-of-bitches get you down."

Jack and Perry left. They climbed into the back of a black automobile and drove away.

Kiko waited on the sidewalk. The skyline stretched against the powder blue sky. He thought he could touch the buildings from where he stood. Cars and busses roared through the streets. Construction crews climbed steel skeletons; cement mixers, trucks and cranes shrieked into the pure air. Hobos stood in line for hours, dancing to sirens and cop whistles. Stray dogs barked at baseball players in the park on Welton; a color television set turned on for the first time in a large house on the edge of the city; the news man talked about the upcoming Sputnik first anniversary. Irish songs and Italian mandolins mixed with the smells of fresh tamales and boiled chitlins. Church bells, synagogue chants and Arapaho drums echoed along the Valley Highway.

Sometimes words don't mean anything at all.

Kiko hung the strap on his shoulder, lifted his box and walked into Denver's heart.

"I'll have to read Jack's book," he said to Duke and Willy.